Unshackled

Rachael Stewart

DEEP DESIRES PRESS

Winnipeg, Canada

Visit http://www.deepdesirespress.com for more scorching hot erotica and erotic romance.

WIN FREE EBOOKS!

Every month, one lucky subscriber to the Deep Desires Press newsletter will win an ebook!

All you have to do is subscribe and you'll be entered every month!

Visit deepdesirespress.com/newsletter to sign up today!

For my very own Andy & Ange,
without your time, honesty and everlasting patience,
I would never have got to this point.
And to all the team at Deep Desires Press,
for taking a chance on me and making this book
the best it can possibly be.
You are all awesome!
Love Rx

Unshackled

Chapter One

I WAS KNEE HIGH IN soiled horse bedding when I first saw her. She was all perfect and pristine and I, filthy and disheveled, with straw in places that didn't bear thinking about.

I couldn't take my eyes from her as she stepped from the sleek black sports car—a gift from Dad, no doubt! I could feel the familiar resentment rising within, along with a degree of curiosity as to why she would be venturing into my domain. None of his playthings ever visited the stables, heaven forbid the smell should ruin their perfume or the muck make it into their heels!

In spite of myself, I continued to watch as one long, lithe leg emerged from the car, followed by another, their beautifully tanned lengths drawing my gaze and holding me captive. The rest of her didn't disappoint. As her body unfolded, my own reacted, a startling warmth spreading through my lower belly as I took in her curvaceous form. Dad had truly outdone himself this time.

She was tall, but then that could be down to the ridiculous stilettos that she wore. Her short, white dress clung to her body like a second skin, flaunting her amazingly pert behind, slim waist, and ample cleavage. As she threw her deep auburn waves over her shoulder, my jaw mentally hit the deck and despite my shameless gawping I found it impossible to tear my eyes away.

But then her gaze settled on me and I died, heat soaring to my cheeks at the mortifying direction of my thoughts. My eyes shot to the floor and I busied myself with the mucking out, praying she would just get about her business and be gone.

"Abi?"

The sound of my name being uttered in her husky English accent did nothing to ease my raging hormones and I tried to ignore her, stabbing my fork back into the straw and tossing it to one side.

"Abi?" she called again. This time I could hear her heels clipping the cobbled paving as she headed toward me.

Letting go of a steadying breath, I rounded on her.

"Hey, mom!" I said sarcastically, regretting it as soon as my eyes lifted to hers, my cocky stance dissipating at her proximity and leaving me feeling nothing but foolish. I was twenty-two after all, not some disgruntled teenager out to do battle with yet another stepmother.

Surprisingly, she smiled, her beautiful face breaking into a wide grin as she removed her fashionably large shades and fixed me with a pair of brilliant green eyes.

"You can call me Emma, I'm not quite mom yet," she purred, toying with the sunglasses in her perfectly manicured hands.

"True." The monosyllable was all I could muster as I continued to squirm before her, my body alarmingly aware of her every inch. What was wrong with me? I wasn't even gay. Or at least I hadn't thought I was. That's a new tale for the shrink! "Shit."

"Sorry?"

I frowned; I hadn't meant to swear aloud. As first meetings went, this was going really well—*not!* "Sorry, I just remembered I was supposed to be somewhere."

Her face fell in obvious disappointment. "Oh."

"Was there something you wanted?" I asked, surprised at her reaction.

"I was hoping you could show me around the stables, your father said you would take me through the stud and find me a match?"

"Stepfather," I corrected instinctively, surprising even myself as the bitterness that normally remained trapped inside at any reference to him came tumbling out.

Aside from the brief narrowing of her eyes, she didn't seem bothered by my momentary lapse of the doting daughter pretense Dad insisted on, instead offering me another tummy-turning smile. "Yes, of course, stepfather."

All sense screamed at me to see her out of my domain—pronto. And yet, the very suggestion that she shared a passion for horses was too much to resist. "You ride?"

"As often as I can."

I took the opportunity to leisurely scan the length of her, a smile now creeping into my lips as I reacquainted myself with her totally impractical ensemble, right down to her baby pink stilettos.

"I have a change of clothes in the trunk," she hurried out, the source of my amusement not lost on her as she dropped the polished façade befitting of her thirty-something years and became almost childlike in her eagerness.

"I guess I can spare half an hour," I said, trying not to sound too keen at the prospect. "Go and grab your things, there's an office you can use to change in."

"Thank you so much!"

I watched as she raced back to the car, her heels not hindering her speed in the slightest and only serving to emphasize the hypnotic wiggle of her hips.

Forcing myself to turn away, I stepped from the straw pile and headed to the entrance of the office, brushing at my clothes in a self-conscious attempt to clean myself up.

She was quick to join me. Her effort not to cause me any extra delay was again surprising. She was turning out to be very different to Dad's usual conquests and no matter how disconcerting, I couldn't deny that I found her attractive. Gay or not, the idea of her soon undressing did things to me that I didn't want to acknowledge.

I swallowed hard, trying to force some normality into my voice. "I'm afraid the office has no curtains..."

She gave me a carefree shrug. "Not a problem, as far as I can see we have the place to ourselves."

I nodded, my voice lost to my racing pulse and wayward imaginings. She strode ahead of me through the office, her confidence in the unfamiliar surroundings both enviable and intensely appealing. As she deposited her bag on the desk and started to pull out her clothes I urged myself to turn away but my body refused. I watched as she took hold of the hem of her dress, my mouth going dry with anticipation and then she paused, turning to look at me over her shoulder, her eyes gleaming provocatively.

The air escaped my lungs in a rush. Fuck! This couldn't be happening.

"I'll just be outside," I blurted, losing my nerve and bolting as quick as I could, almost taking the nearby coat stand with me. How smooth...not!

What was wrong with me? Dad had brought many a pretty woman home since Mum passed away almost fifteen years ago. And these days, most of them weren't even that much older than me. Yet this one was different. She was stirring up desires that normally only my vivid imagination and saucy novels could spark. Even the odd stable hand and past boyfriends hadn't caused such a throbbing reaction on sight. And never before had a woman inspired such an interest. But this one...my eyes were drawn to the window as I chanced a glance.

I could just make out the flash of white fabric being tossed across the desk before my eyes focused fully on the interior and her glorious, naked form came into view. She wore nothing but a scanty, white thong. Tan lines notably absent. Hot liquid pooled unashamedly between my legs, the intensity of my reaction startling me into looking away.

But I couldn't help myself. Pressing up against the outer wall of the office, my gaze drifted back, first to her face as I prayed she wouldn't see me. I needn't have worried; her attention was fixed entirely on the contents of her bag. I could feel the thrill spread through me as I relished the unhindered view, my breath catching in my throat as I took in her bare breasts. So full, they defied gravity as the pert center of each small rosebud pointed upward, begging to be touched, licked, fondled...I bit my upper lip as the thought of enjoying each peak raced through my mind—

"Abi!"

The sound of her calling my name made me jump out of my skin. My eyes shot to her face but she was looking toward the door, completely oblivious to my watchful gaze.

"Yes?" I called, trying to sound normal while my pulse raced out of control and my eyes were once again drawn to her body, her breasts moving hypnotically as she returned to rummage through her bag.

"Do you have a shirt I can borrow? I don't seem to have one." She scooped up a black sports bra and began fastening it around herself. "Abi?" she said, pausing her movements to listen out for me.

God, I needed to get a grip. What was it she wanted? A shirt!

"Err, yeah, sure, one sec." Tearing myself away, I headed to the boot room, my whole body throbbing with an awakened need that I desperately wanted to satisfy.

Could I? Right here and now? It wouldn't take long, of that I was certain. It really would be torture to spend the next half hour with her in this heightened state of need.

It was true that there was no one else around, and the boot room was closed off completely. One way in, one way out. Mind made up, I entered the room and closed the door behind me. Leaning back against it, I wasted no time in loosening the fly on my jeans and thrust my hand into my panties, amazed at just how wet I was. A small groan escaped my lips as I pulled back over my clit, savoring the sensation. Oh yes! I was so ready.

All hesitation gone, I circled the nub, gently at first and then harder, reveling in the heat spreading through my body. My mind filled with the image of her naked form as I imagined the feel of those breasts beneath my hands, my mouth, my tongue...

I spread my legs wide to gain better access, my rhythm picking up a pace as my whole body began to tense up. I was so wet and so close. My other hand shoved up into my bra to release one aching breast, the cold air hitting the nipple as I groped at the flesh and pinched at the tip. And then I was imagining it was her on me, her mouth, her hands...

"Fuck!" I exploded, my whole body racked with glorious convulsions as my orgasm took hold and sent my legs buckling beneath me.

"Abi, you there?"

Her voice came from the other side of the door. Please, God, don't let her have heard me come!

I took a steadying breath and straightened up, still pinning the door closed.

"Coming!" I called out; I was lucid enough to see the humor in that rather apt response.

Righting my jeans, I grabbed a shirt from the peg and opened the door. I was so grateful for my release, else the sight that greeted me would have tipped me over the edge. Clad only in tight-fitting jodhpurs, riding boots, and sports bra, she looked ready for a raunchy *Playboy* photo shoot, her toned abs glistening in the heat of the day, her hair pulled back in a single tie at the base of her neck. She was totally fuckable and couldn't be any more out of my league, even if she was gay and more importantly, wasn't engaged to my stepfather.

"Here," I said, offering her the shirt.

"You okay?" She was studying me intently, concern etched in her features. "You look very flushed, perhaps you need to get out of the sun for a bit. We could always do this later."

Flushed! I bet I did. I was bound to be sporting my post-romp glow!

"No, I'm fine," I said quickly, wanting to change the subject, "I'm just going to grab a drink, you want something?"

"Yes, please."

She took the shirt from my outstretched hand but her eyes held me hostage, their green depths flashing with some unknown thought that I tried to discern. And then I lost myself in that look; the air filling with a palpable tension as her interest became apparent, her gaze turning hot and hungry. She wanted me!

"You have lovely honey-toned hair," she said softly, reaching out with her free hand to toy with a loose strand.

Every nerve ending in my body rushed to the touch. I could feel the heat rise in my cheeks once again and saw her smile in response, obviously enjoying the visible effect she was having on me. She knew what she was doing, that was quite clear.

She watched me intently as her fingers traveled the length of the strand, her hand brushing over my left breast with the move. My breathing halted as my nipple hardened against the fabric of my bra, lavishing in the fleeting contact.

"Is it highlighted?" she asked innocently, moving to repeat the caress with another strand of hair.

"Natural," I breathed.

The ache between my legs returned tenfold, my breasts tingling in desperate anticipation of her next stroke...

"You're much more beautiful than your father...sorry, stepfather...gives you credit for."

I reacted as though slapped, her words sending ice through my veins as the reminder of who she was and the man she was marrying hit home. Stepping back to break the contact, I folded my arms across my chest and dropped my gaze.

"I'm sorry—" she began.

"I'll just get those drinks," I bit out, taking a wide berth around her and heading to the office fridge.

It was no surprise that Dad had spoken critically of me, that hadn't bothered me in the slightest. No, it was fear of what that man would do if he discovered this attraction between us. Thank God, my next shrink appointment was scheduled for tomorrow; hopefully he would help me make sense of my crazy thoughts and raging hormones. I just needed to get through today first.

Chapter Two

Two HOURS LATER, WE CAME thundering through the stables, the horses' hooves pounding the ground at a speed to match my elevated heart rate.

She was an accomplished rider, successfully beating me back to the stables. As my horse rounded up behind her, she swung her leg over Storm, the gray Arabian horse she had taken to riding, and dismounted. She paused to give him an affectionate pat before leading him to the water trough. I followed her lead, my eyes not once leaving her captivating figure.

"Sorry to have kept you from your plans. I hadn't realized how late it was," she said, glancing up at me as I joined her; she looked more beautiful than ever. Her cheeks flushed from the exertion, her eyes glittering brightly. "I had such a great time."

"Me too," I said easily. And I had. More fun than I'd had in ages. She was a breath of fresh air in an otherwise glamorous yet downright boring existence. Added to that, the sexual awareness she evoked in me was like a drug that I couldn't get enough of. Her carefree manner with the horses, her knowledge of the animal, her willingness to get down and dirty, all served to intensify her appeal.

"Can we ride again soon?" she asked, eagerly.

"Sure."

Our gazes locked, the unspoken chemistry passing between us once again, her eyes scanned my face and tentatively she moved toward me. My hands itched to reach for her but then she froze, her eyes flicking away to focus behind me.

"Darling," she called, her English accent perfectly apparent once again.

"There you are!" came my stepfather's unmistakable voice, his tone mildly admonishing.

Turning around, I watched him approach. Sunglasses masking his expression, he was every bit the mature playboy in his dark, designer suit and crisp, white shirt, unbuttoned at the collar. His deep brown hair, overlong for his age, was slicked back, the hint of gray at his temples the only real sign of his advancing years.

"Daddy," I said dutifully in greeting.

He threw me a derisive glare. "What is the point in having you schooled in dressage to have you turn out like some tramp?"

I opened my mouth to deliver a sharp retort but promptly shut it again, Emma's apologetic gaze stopping me in my tracks. She needn't have bothered feeling bad on my behalf. I'd given up on a kind word from him long ago.

"I've been looking for you everywhere," he said, his focus returning to Emma. "I have some friends that are eager to meet you."

"Sorry, darling," she said, closing the distance between them and giving him a chaste kiss on the cheek. "I totally lost track of time, Abi has done a wonderful job looking after me."

"I should hope so, it's the least she could do since this lot costs me a fortune to run. Speaking of which"—he gestured to my straw-covered clothing in disgust—"have you been mucking out again?"

I shrugged. "I like doing it."

"For God's sake, Abi, that's what I pay people for! Do you always have to be such an embarrassment?" He threw his hand in the air in exasperation and turned to Emma. "Come, they're waiting for us."

Taking Emma by the elbow, he flicked his gaze back to me just long enough to state, "Dinner's at seven and make an effort!"

I scowled at his retreating form, angrier than I can remember, the realization dawning that it was down to how he had belittled me in front of Emma that had upset me most.

Well, make an effort I would. But not for his benefit...

Six-thirty came and I was pacing the floor. Having spent the last two hours fussing over my appearance, I was now early and a bag of nerves. Striding to the bedroom mirror for the umpteenth time, I assessed my reflection.

I'd opted for a black, sleeveless jumpsuit with a deep plunging neckline. It was borderline indecent really, but the exquisite cut and fabric screamed designer and made it perfect for tonight's affair. I'd curled my hair and pinned it in a tousled up-do. My face, tanned from being outdoors so much, had a healthy-looking glow, the blue depths of my eyes popping amidst the smoky effect of the eye shadow I'd applied and my lips glistening with a baby pink gloss that matched Emma's cute, if impractical shoes from earlier in the day. Just the thought of her sent butterflies through my tummy. I was anxious, yet beyond excited about seeing her again.

A knock at the door drew my attention.

"Come in."

Lily, the housekeeper, entered, her step faltering slightly as she took in my appearance. "Why, Miss Sawyer, you're simply stunning!"

I smiled at her genuine compliment. "Thank you, Lily."

"Your father is asking for you to join him and Miss Jones for pre-dinner drinks."

"Sounds lovely," I said, trying to ignore the surge of nerves that gnawed away at my insides. "I'll just get some shoes."

"Very well, Miss Sawyer." She turned on her heel and left the room.

I slipped on a pair of sparkly flats and followed closely behind her, checking my appearance at every opportunity on the way, trying to reassure myself that I looked good.

No amount of mental encouragement could have prepared me for my encounter with Emma though. As I entered the room and caught sight of her before the fireplace, a rush of desire flooded me along with a feeling of total inadequacy. Even from behind she was breathtaking. She wore a full-length red dress, the back to which was practically non-existent as it dipped to form a curve just above her pert behind before dropping gracefully to the floor. Her hair fell in loose waves across her back, teasing me with flashes of her bare skin and sending my mouth dry.

As she turned to greet me, my inner turmoil heightened at the appreciation I could see mirrored in her eyes. What must have been a second passed, yet it felt like an eternity as our eyes openly enjoyed one another.

"Abi," she said eventually, placing her drink on the mantle and sweeping toward me.

I smiled in response but my legs refused to budge. As she came to stand before me, she took hold of my arms and leaned in to kiss my cheek. Her touch ricocheted through me like a fire bolt, her perfume filling my senses, intoxicating me and drawing my head inwards to bring her lips closer to my own. The move was so subtle it was doubtful that anyone else would notice, but as my gaze locked with hers, I could see she had.

"Seems you can look halfway decent after all, Abi."

My stepfather's words shattered the moment and I almost leapt from Emma's embrace.

"Daddy," I said turning in his direction and grabbing an untouched glass of bubbles from the awaiting tray, knocking back a great, big gulp.

He followed the move but didn't reproach me for it.

"To what do I owe this pre-dinner drink?" I asked, trying to sound normal and failing miserably.

He eyed me, his gaze probing as he took in my flustered demeanor. "I have a boy coming tonight, his name's Daniel Scott."

My mood sunk as his words hit home and I realized the true purpose of my presence this evening.

"I'd like the two of you to get to know each other better," he continued, his eyes still coldly assessing. "However, you seem out of sorts this evening, perhaps you should go—"

"No!" I blurted out, too quickly. There was no way he was excluding me this evening, regardless of his opportunistic matchmaking. Taking a breath to calm my elevated heart rate, I tried to explain away my behavior. "I'm fine, Daddy, I just got dressed in rather a hurry and feel flustered."

He didn't look convinced and I realized for the first time that it was more than simply displeasure with me that had him concerned, he was on edge in general. Was tonight really such a big deal?

I gestured to the glass in my hand and assured him, "I will be fine after a couple of these."

"You'd better," he said, the words and the vehemence with which he spoke answering my unspoken question. Something major hung in the balance...

"Daniel's father is also coming," he continued, "and not only is the man influential in his own right but he moves in circles that we have yet to venture into. A personal tie to his family is a crucial move for us."

I could sense Emma's gaze on me, concern radiating from her. I really didn't need her sympathy; this was just the way my life was. I would always be a pawn in my stepfather's constant quest to succeed.

"Sure thing," I said, taking another large swig to quash my mounting nerves.

"I also have my lawyer, James, who you know, and his wife coming. All you need to do is make sure Daniel is well tended to and we will take care of the rest."

My skin crawled at the reference to James; the sleazebag really gave me the creeps with his wandering eye. The man thought his looks and wealth meant that he could leer at whomever he chose, whenever he chose. Maybe my presence wasn't such a great idea after all. But giving my stepfather the satisfaction of admitting to being out of my depth didn't appeal in the slightest. So I nodded my agreement and instead focused on downing the remainder of my drink.

Spying the empty glass, my stepfather took the bottle from the ice bucket and began topping it up, using the opportunity to give me a warning glare that clearly said "Do *not* fuck this up for me...or else".

Fear prickled down my spine as our eyes locked, just how big a deal could this be? I mean really, what was the worst that could happen?

The sensation of something cold trickling over my hand cut short my thoughts and I lowered my gaze, mortified to see that the glass shook in my unsteady grip, making it impossible for Dad to pour the drink cleanly.

Forcing my hand still, I lifted my eyes to face off the ferocity of his and tried to smile. "Thank you."

"Darling?" Emma's soft voice broke through the tension, her hand moving to rest on my father's arm. "Perhaps you can take me through your plans for the evening? I want to make sure I do all I can to assist."

Her attempt to draw the focus away from me was a godsend and I flashed her an appreciative smile. She returned it, concern evident in her beautiful green eyes before she looked back to my stepfather and coaxed him away.

I felt uneasy watching them. The sight of Emma's hand on him made me feel queasy and I realized that I was jealous. I studied her as they chatted, her face one of adoration as she listened intently to what he was saying. How could a person of her beauty and quality fall for a man like him? She had to be in it for the lifestyle he could offer. The idea of her having genuine feelings for him was too preposterous to believe and only incited further jealousy. I downed my drink and picked up the bottle for another. This was going to be one long night...

Chapter Three

To SAY THAT I WAS slightly inebriated by the time dinner arrived would probably have been an understatement. But I couldn't work out whether it was the drink going to my head or the jealousy that coursed through my veins at watching Emma flirt with my stepfather. And with James and Diana for that matter. The four chatted intimately with Daniel's father being graced with their attention at regular intervals so as not to leave him out. Daniel and I were simply left to make our own entertainment.

Poor guy too. Although appealing in an athletic jock kind of a way, Daniel was just way too boring. He seemed incapable of any discussion outside the track and field, he clearly had no intellectual qualities, and saw hard work as a thing "the grown-ups" did. His father had obviously given him an easy ride in life and coupled with his sporting ability, his brain had yet to be tested. Still, he found me interesting enough if his avid attention was anything to go on and that meant I was in good stead to please my stepfather.

"What say you, Abi?"

The question came from the man himself, Dad. All heads turned to me expectantly and all I could do was stare back blankly.

"You'll have to excuse my daughter, she may be a beauty but her mind leaves something to be desired," he said, the humor in his voice not quite meeting his eyes. He wasn't impressed at my lack of attention.

The men around the table jeered, except for Daniel who had taken my distraction to mean that I was very much into him and what he had been saying. Poor sap.

"She certainly isn't cut from the same cloth as you, Edward," Diana said to my stepfather, the flirtatious purr to her voice delivering the insult with ease and causing my hackles to rise. *Bitch!*

"Well, we can't all be as perfect as the acclaimed businessman Edward Sawyer, else life would be boring." My voice dripped with sarcasm but I was past caring.

My stepfather's gaze narrowed on me, the pulse working in his jaw the only sign of his simmering temper. "I was suggesting, *Abigail*, that you take Daniel for a nightcap."

The way he stressed my name was all the warning I needed, the last time he had said it in such a way he had delivered me the ass spanking of a lifetime. And it wasn't like he had done it in private either. After catching me fucking one of the stable hands he had yanked my bare body right out from under the guy, bent me over right there and then, and spanked me until I cried. It was his way of making sure the dude never came near me again. And then rather than sack the guy, he made sure he stayed on as a constant reminder of my shame and as a warning message to anyone else who showed any sign of interest. The humiliation was enough to send heat to my cheeks once more and I took up my drink, keen to remain composed.

"No problem, Daddy."

He twitched at my sickly sweet reference, but seemed happier that I was on side once more.

"I don't expect that we will see you later, we have quite a bit of business still to discuss and the ladies have lots to catch up on," he looked from Emma to Diana as he said the latter and I followed his gaze. The two women shared a look that made me uncomfortable but I couldn't fathom why. I was over-sensitive for sure.

"Like I said, no problem." I pushed myself up from the table and deposited my napkin. Part of me didn't want to leave the room. Or rather, didn't want to leave Emma. The other part felt completely out of place in their company. "Come Daniel, I'll show you just what Daddy's cellar has to offer—"

"Ah, avoid the cellar, Abi," my stepfather hurried out unexpectedly, "that stuff is reserved for special occasions."

I looked at him, puzzled. He loved to show off his drinks collection. This evening seemed like the perfect opportunity.

He didn't elaborate however and ultimately I couldn't really care less what we drank. Drink was drink.

"I'll take the decanter from the side then."

Not waiting for a response, I grabbed the said booze along with two fresh glasses and made for the door. Daniel was beside me in a second, his eagerness for some "alone time" more than apparent.

Robert, Daniel's father, eyed us both, his face breaking into a wide grin as he said, "Don't forget we're setting off early tomorrow, son; try and get some sleep, won't you?"

Heat crept into my cheeks at his meaning. Some people had no decency. My eyes flicked to Emma who was watching me, her expression unreadable. Did she know how badly I wanted to be with her instead? Why was Dad so keen to palm her off with Diana? The two women had only just met. But if I was honest, it was the tone in which he had referred to them "catching up" that bothered me. There was a sexual undertone, of that I was certain...

"Thanks for that, Dad," Daniel said, in mock gratitude and then he gestured to the doorway. "Shall we?"

Shifting my attention from Emma, I nodded and with more cheer than I felt, I bid them goodnight and headed for the door.

"I'm sorry about my father, he can be a bit brash at times," Daniel said once we were out of earshot.

"No need to apologize, I know exactly how it feels to be shown up by one's illustrious father, stepfather or otherwise."

"Seems we do have something in common then?"

I glanced at him sharply, concerned that he had picked up on our lack of connection but his eyes danced with amusement and I couldn't help but smile. His honesty was both welcome and refreshing.

"Let's take this to the terrace and see what other similarities we can uncover," I said, making the statement intentionally provocative. I was in the mood for some fun, anything to keep my mind from the worrying direction of my thoughts.

"Sounds good to me."

I led us through the halls to the back of the house where the doors opened onto the terrace. Pushing them ajar, I gestured for Daniel to precede me.

"You're quite the modern woman," he said, picking up on my typically masculine gesture.

I shrugged and stepped out. The warm night air hit me full force, its freshness mixing with the alcohol in my blood and causing my footing to falter.

"Here." Daniel was quick to take up my arm and remove the bottle and glassware from my hand.

"Thanks," I said, dropping into a nearby sun lounger and kicking off my shoes. I could feel the stress leave my body as I sunk into the plushness of the bed and basked in the soft orange glow of the disappearing sun.

"Wow, that is something special."

Daniel's comment drew my attention. He was staring out at the far-reaching countryside, his gaze serene as he faced off the sunset. He looked younger, less hard. His features softened by the low light, his brown eyes taking on its honey glow and mirroring the color of his hair. He really was quite handsome and in the intimacy of our beautiful surroundings I could feel the stirrings of desire spark within me.

Plus, he was right. Before us, the countryside stretched as far as the eye could see, completely unspoiled by the trappings of the modern world. It formed a breathtaking backdrop to the kidney-shaped pool and sun terrace on which we sat. I couldn't help the sigh that escaped me as I acknowledged this was one of the reasons I stuck around...

"It is," I said softly.

My words drew his gaze. "And yet you sound so sad?"

I couldn't make out from his words whether his question was born of concern or scorn but experience told me it was the latter.

"I know what you're thinking: dumb, spoiled rich girl, doesn't know she's born," I rushed out.

He dropped to the lounger next to me and placed his hand atop my own, cutting off my outburst. "Not at all! Christ, if anyone can understand what it's like to be a part of this world yet feel utterly alone, it's me."

I eyed him as though seeing him properly for the first time, both inside and out, and the loneliness I felt inside combusted with the sudden heat of desire. I wanted him, right here and now. I wanted the complete abandonment and utter distraction of a wild sexual encounter. But I couldn't. My mind was a mess and the alcohol was making it hard to think straight. I raised my eyes to his, about to say something but the heat I saw in his gaze stopped me. He wanted me just as much as I wanted him.

"You know, we could take this somewhere more private," he suggested, his tone low.

I wanted to, I really did. But the sensible part of me, the part that realized alcohol wasn't the best aid when it came to embarking on new friendships of any kind, was still with me.

Spying my hesitation, he picked up the bottle and poured us both a drink. "Or we can just drink up and enjoy the view?"

I nodded, relief sweeping through me. "For now," I agreed, raising my glass to his and settling back into the bed.

He mirrored my position on his own lounger and we lay there watching the sunset, conversation flowing between us freely now that we were alone. I asked him about his training and he quizzed me on my riding. Knowing what made him tick made passing the time easy and as each drink flowed through me, the sexual awareness began to mount. By the time we had polished off the last of the decanter, my mind was made up.

"How about I get us another and we take it upstairs?" I said, propping myself up on my side so that I could lean toward him.

He copied my move, stopping with his mouth mere inches from my own, his heated gaze falling to my lips. "Sounds like a mighty fine idea."

I knew he was going to kiss me, I could see the intent in his eyes and my nerve endings tingled in anticipation, eager for his touch. As he dropped his mouth to mine, I parted my lips willingly, waiting for the invasion of his own. And yet he hovered just above me, the move purposefully hesitant as he waited on my lead.

He needn't have worried, yet his concern was sweet and destroyed any remaining hesitation I may have felt. Tilting my head back, my lips met with his and I moaned aloud at the contact.

The sound was all the encouragement he needed. Shifting his body onto my lounger, he pressed up against me, his mouth moving hungrily over mine. I matched him move for move, my leg hooking over his hips to allow his burgeoning erection to press against me. My hands moved roughly through his hair as my lower body began to rock against him in a fevered quest for satisfaction. His hands roamed over my front, desperately seeking access to my breasts, my nipples hardening at the prospect, the sensation almost painful at the prolonged wait as he struggled to navigate the jumpsuit.

"Blasted thing," he cursed, shifting our entwined bodies so that he could take hold of the zip at my back.

What semblance of sanity I had left surfaced and I took hold of his hand. "Not here."

He rested his head against my own, fighting for control. "You're right," he breathed eventually.

"Come on." Moving off the sun lounger, I slipped on my shoes and pulled him with me. "We can stop at Daddy's cellar on the way."

The house was unusually quiet. I had expected to hear some sounds echoing through the halls from the dinner party but there was nothing.

We headed down a level, passing the kitchen and utility to pause before the door that led to the cellar.

"I'll be back shortly, any preference for red or white?" I asked, turning to face him, excitement coursing through me as I took in his disheveled appearance at my hands, his eyes ablaze with a need I had generated. Tonight wasn't going so bad after all.

"Whatever you fancy."

I reached up on tiptoes and planted a lingering kiss on his lips before opening the door and heading down the steps.

It didn't take long to realize that I wasn't alone. The faint sound of music reached my ears along with the gentle hum of voices. The cellar consisted of a few rooms with a corridor running the length of them. Most rooms possessed viewing windows, a way for *Daddy Dearest* to observe his stores without having to disturb the inner temperatures or some such nonsense. The sounds were coming from the largest of the rooms, which housed a central stage with a table for his wine tasting demonstrations.

So this was why he hadn't wanted me down here. Curiosity sufficiently aroused, I slipped off my shoes and crept to the window. The room was softly lit. Robert and James were lounging in one of the deep sofas that adorned the stonewalled room. My stepfather stood at the bar pouring drinks and at the heart of the room, leaning up against the table were Emma and Diana, enjoying what looked to be an intimate conversation. Even from this distance, I could sense the sudden closeness between them and I didn't like it.

My stepfather moved from the bar and I leapt back for fear of being spotted. I could hear my heart pounding in my ears and I knew I should take a bottle and leave. But I couldn't; this was no ordinary wine tasting session my stepfather was hosting, of that I was certain.

Risking another look, I watched him take up a seat with the other men, all three now with their backs to me, their attention fully on the stage. Diana passed Emma her half-finished wine glass and lifted herself to sit at the edge of the table. Taking up her own glass, Emma moved away to place their drinks on the other end of the table and when she turned back, the air left my lungs at the sultry look in her eye.

Slowly, she moved toward Diana, her hand trailing the edge of the table, her eyes fixed on the other woman as a slight smile played about her lips. She looked completely at home in this arrangement and I didn't want or care to think about that right now.

Looking back to Diana, I was surprised to see how nervous she looked, her knees pinned together, her expression almost wary as she watched the other woman progress toward her. Her uneasiness wasn't lost on Emma either. As she came to pause before her, she cocked her head to one side and slowly mouthed the word "relax".

Diana gave her a half smile in response, her legs slackening marginally as her eyes dropped to Emma's delectable lips that were no more than a foot away.

"That's better," Emma said in approval as she slowly leaned inwards, her tongue flicking out to moisten her bottom lip just as she sipped at Diana's upturned mouth. The move was fleeting, yet the thrill that coursed through me was like nothing I'd ever experienced. I didn't want to blink for fear of missing a thing. Even the jealousy sparking within wasn't enough to ruin the fire in my veins.

I watched in avid fascination as Diana's eyes fluttered closed and she offered her mouth up to Emma's once more, her hands falling to her sides as she surrendered herself up to the other woman's attentions. And Emma didn't disappoint; as her hands slipped up and over Diana's thighs, the girl melted before her, her legs falling open to grant access beneath the fabric of her dress, her head lolling back as her lips parted on a soft moan.

Emma smiled her approval, her gaze turning heated and hungry. I couldn't breathe I was so turned on, the ache between my legs painfully intense. I willed Emma's hands upward, I willed her to expose Diana's body to me, I willed her to do all manner of things to the girl for my enjoyment. I was beyond reproach right now, all thoughts of the other men in the room, of Daniel upstairs, had evaporated as my body and mind gave itself up to the scene before me.

Chapter Four

THE FACT THAT I WANTED to be the focus of Emma's attention still gnawed at me but even that couldn't spoil my enjoyment.

I watched in jealous fascination as she slid Diana's dress up to her hips and coaxed the girl's behind forward so that her lower body pressed against her own. Her hands now moving to her hair, she pulled Diana's head back to lick and nip at her exposed throat. And Diana relished every bit, her head shifting side to side as she encouraged Emma to enjoy more and more of her creamy skin, her lower body instinctively beginning to writhe against the friction provided by Emma's form.

I waited with bated breath for the girls' mouths to meet again, but each time they got close Emma would break away, seemingly teasing Diana, or the men, or both. As Diana attempted to claim Emma's mouth once more, Emma yanked at her hair, forcing her head back to break the contact. The girl cried out, her frustration escalating along with the tempo of her pulsating body. Emma simply smiled, her total control and lack of mercy so mind-blowingly erotic as she dipped her head to nuzzle at the sensitive skin beneath the girl's earlobe.

Diana's breathing started to become a pant, her desperation for release fueling my own need. As Emma brought her free hand up to cup Diana's jawline, the girl instinctively moved into the caress. Her lips claiming Emma's fingers and doing what she so desperately wanted to do with her tongue, she tasted, teased, and sucked with such a hunger that it wasn't long before Emma could no longer resist the draw of Diana's mouth.

Breaking away from the girl's neck, she replaced her finger with her tongue and they lapped at one another, their dainty, pink tongues interlocking with such frenzy; twisting, flicking, tasting...it was like no kiss I'd ever seen, let alone experienced, and the dampness spread thick and fast between my legs—Christ, they were hot! I could have come just watching their exposed tongues enjoy one another, but then Emma shifted, her hand tugging hard on Diana's hair once more and forcing her to lose her balance. The girl fell back against the table, her elbows planting to support her upper body.

Emma paused to enjoy the view of Diana's wanton body spread before her, her face flushed with excitement, her enjoyment at the power she yielded over the girl more than apparent.

"Please," Diana said, her plea only just audible through the glass pane but her desperation unmistakable.

Emma smiled provocatively and moved her hands to trace a slow path along the neckline of Diana's dress, her heated gaze intent on Diana's.

"You want me?" Emma asked softly, teasingly.

"Yes," Diana whispered, the sound lost through the wall of the cellar but her assent clear.

"Here?" Emma asked, her hands moving over her clothes to cup her breasts, her thumbs circling each hardened center.

Diana threw her head back, moaning with delight, and I bit my lip for fear of the sound being echoed by myself.

Emma's hands then moved to the buttons of Diana's dress and one by one she released them, pausing to caress the girl's bare skin as she went. By the time she had unveiled the full length of Diana's trim body, the girl was writhing uncontrollable, teetering on the edge of coming.

"I didn't take you as someone with voyeuristic tendencies."

Shit! Daniel! I spun on my heel. He was directly behind me, his gaze fixed very much on me. How long had he been there!

"Sorry!" I whispered, my mind racing with what I should do. Usher him away or—

"What has you so enraptured?" he said quietly, taking his lead from me and lowering his voice.

"You wouldn't believe it," I said, turning back to the window. I felt him come up behind me, his head resting above my own.

"Well, I'll be damned, now I can see why you weren't quick to return."

I needn't have worried about his reaction, the obvious awakening of his cock pressing into my backside was enough to put my mind at rest, he was enjoying the scene just as much as me.

"You are completely forgiven," he said, his tone distracted. "Fuck, you must be so wet right now..."

I nodded; the incessant ache between my legs throbbing so desperately that I had to squeeze my thighs tight to nurse it.

"I can help you with that..." His voice rumbled low against my ear, his lips brushing against my lobe as he pressed me up against the wall. I felt his hands at the zipper of my jumpsuit, high up my back and I had to stop myself crying out with relief that release would soon be mine. That this crazy, unprecedented passion would soon be sated.

Before me, Diana's dress had been tossed to one side and Emma was tracing the outline of each nipple as they protruded through the fabric of her black lace bra. I was so desperate to see her breasts stripped of the confines of her underwear that I didn't even blink, my focus intent on the movement of Emma's hands as she finally slid her palms beneath the cups and lifted the delicious mounds from the material, exposing the gloriously naked flesh to my appreciative gaze. They were fuller than Emma's, the nipples darker, the skin flushed with her abundant desire.

A moan erupted from me unbidden and I clamped down on my lip to rein it in.

"What is it, baby?" Daniel whispered into my ear.

Christ, she was beautiful. They both were.

Emma began to massage one gloriously full mound while expertly toying with the peak at the other. Envy coursed through me anew, as my body begged to be in the thick of the scene before me.

"Do you want some of that?" Daniel continued, his voice gruff against my ear sending delightful shivers down my spine.

Without waiting for my response, his hands moved to my shoulders and he shoved the fabric of my jumpsuit down until the straps hung from my wrists. I was now naked to my thighs, save for my thong. My lack of bra a relief as the cold air swept over each aching nipple and encircled my upper body, every nerve ending heightened in my desperate state of need. I wanted so badly for him to fuck me. And hard.

I was vaguely aware of him rustling a packet behind me and realized with some gratitude that he was putting on a condom. At least one of us had some sense left. Before I knew it, he was back, pressing me up against the cold wall, my bare nipples scraping the rough surface causing me to cry out at the ripples of pleasure it sent through me.

Shit! That was loud. Panicking, I scanned the room before me, praying I hadn't been heard. But the sound of me had been drowned out by the cries from Diana; the girl was so close to the brink. Her head thrown back in pure ecstasy, her now naked form arched back over the table as Emma nipped and sucked at each breast in turn whilst her hand dipped between the girl's legs.

Daniel pulled at my thong, tugging it into a tight string against my crotch, the sensation painfully erotic and I cried out again, writhing against the fabric. His other hand came at me from behind, seeking out the entrance to my pussy.

"God, you are so wet, baby."

I started to rock against him, reveling in the friction of my still-present panties and his probing fingers. All the while, my gaze transfixed on Emma and her skilled assault on the other girl's body, her mouth now replacing her fingers to feast on the naked valley between Diana's legs.

And then one of the men moved. It was James. He approached the women, his hand working at his crotch. What was he doing? He couldn't be about to fuck Emma, surely not...

"Remember, James, the ass. The pussy is all mine."

The order came from my stepfather and I watched with horrified fascination as James acknowledged his words with a greedy smile, his hands moving to lift Emma's dress to massage her naked behind.

Emma barely glanced up from her position. Diana looked though. Her hungry gaze fixed on her husband as she watched him position himself and thrust his cock forward. Emma cried out, and I could swear she was in pain, but then the sound changed, pleasure ringing through as her body relaxed into his rhythm.

"Don't...don't stop," Emma begged, throwing James a heated look over her shoulder.

I had never witnessed anything so hot in my life. As she returned her attention to Diana, I reveled in the sight of the growing sexual tension building in their bodies.

"Your turn, baby..." Daniel said behind me, shoving my thong down and maneuvering his cock against my entrance, his hand returning to take up a joyous tempo over my clit.

God, yes, take me already! I wanted to scream at him. Instead, I thrust myself backward, down onto his hard shaft and almost exploded there and then.

"Steady, baby," he ground out, pinning my hips with his hands to prevent me from moving over him. "Let's enjoy this with them."

I squirmed beneath his grip, showing rather than telling him that I needed release. And now!

Slowly, he pulled out and I heard him groan low in his throat just as a huge cry rang out from Diana. The girl's body convulsed as her climax overcame her, each wave sending her body into a spasm as Emma pinioned her legs apart and watched her release with carnal satisfaction.

As the waves subsided, her body relaxed into the table and she stretched out languorously while Emma rocked above her with each continued thrust from James.

"Now don't be selfish, Diana," James said, his voice rough with growing tension as he slowed his movements to regain some control. "I think you should return the favor."

Diana's sated expression quickly evolved to one of hunger as she propped herself up onto her elbows and nodded.

"Take off her dress, darling," she commanded, her gaze fixed on Emma as she moistened her upper lip with her dainty pink tongue.

James did as she bid, lifting the fabric over Emma's head; his cock still nestled in Emma's sweet cheeks. As he unveiled her heavenly, sweat-covered body, Daniel's pace increased; she clearly had the same effect on him, his control was slipping.

I watched transfixed as Diana slid off the table to kneel between the legs of the entwined couple. Her hands lifting to cup and toy with her husband's balls and then her head tilted back so that she could bury her mouth between Emma's legs. Emma cried out at the contact, throwing her head back in pure pleasure.

"She's good, isn't she?" James said hoarsely, his hands moving to grope Emma's breasts as he picked up his tempo against her.

Daniel followed suit, his body plowing into me, my breasts scraping the wall with each move. I clamped my teeth down into my lip to prevent me crying out again as my whole body turned rigid with my impending climax. Before me, I could see both Emma and James reach a crescendo in unison just as I exploded, every bit of me racked with such a ferocious orgasm—

"Fuck!" Daniel swore as he thrust into me one last time.

To my horror, Robert and my stepfather both turned in our direction and I flung us back against the wall, praying they hadn't seen us.

"Quick, we need to go!" I whispered, pulling my suit back up over my arms.

Daniel nodded, flashing me an apologetic look and we fled up the stairs, back into the main body of the house.

Seconds passed and there was no indication we had been followed. Daniel suddenly started to laugh and I couldn't help but join him, relief at not getting caught unhinging us both.

"We should do this again some time," he said between laughs.

"It's not a typical evening under this roof, I assure you." At least not that I was aware! But there was no denying the familiarity of the whole setup for my stepfather and no one had been surprised at the goings on in that room, least of all Emma. "I'm going to take a shower, you can crash in my bed, it's where they expect you to be, after all."

"Sounds good, especially since you may want a repeat." He winked at me but I was past it. As much as I had enjoyed the evening, my feelings toward Emma were starting to worry me big time. It was a good job my scheduled shrink appointment was set for tomorrow morning, I was going to need it.

"Follow me, " I said, and taking his hand I led him up the stairs to my room.

Thankfully, my overlong shower was suitably lengthy that Daniel was out for the count by the time I returned. He looked like he'd fallen asleep midway through undressing. His body lay sprawled atop the covers, shirt undone to the waist, trousers still belted and shoes on. His exposed, muscular chest rising and falling with each heavy breath, his head flopped to the side between two pillows.

Taking pity on him, I stripped his shoes and socks and moved to remove his belt. As the metal buckle jangled in my hands, I felt a surprising stirring between my legs and instinctively was drawn to the soft mound below. Tentatively I stroked the area, fascinated as it pulsed beneath my touch. Could I really turn him on whilst asleep? I stroked again and sure enough, the member twitched under the attention. This was wrong. But it felt good. Powerful even. Entranced, I toyed with the length of him, enjoying how his cock twitched upward as my fingers reached the tip.

Keen to see more of him, I unzipped his pants and shimmied them off. He stirred at the movement and I told myself it was fine, I was simply making sure he was comfy after all and I waited to see if he was going to wake. But his steady breathing resumed, his body relaxing once again into the covers.

Gaining in confidence, I straddled his thighs and moved my hand over the bulge, watching with awe as it started to grow further beneath my touch. As it reached its solid state I could resist no more and opened his briefs, his cock leaping free into my awaiting hand, eager for attention. Before I'd even thought on it, my mouth was wrapped around him and I was sucking, long and hard. I heard him groan, a guttural cry, and I knew then he was awake.

"Christ, Abi!"

Then his hands were in my hair, roughly tugging and pressing as he forced me into a rhythm of his choosing. I could feel the wetness leaking down my inner thighs as my body once again sought fulfillment. Lowering my hand to cover my clit, I began to rub myself just as he exploded into my mouth, his seed filling me, and hungrily I swallowed it down. His release was enough to spur my own and I came hard, falling forward to rest my head on his solid torso as the spasms took control of me.

When my body finally relaxed, he reached down and pulled me onto his chest, mumbling into my hair. "God, baby, you're something else."

I was asleep in seconds, sated and too exhausted to think.

Chapter Five

As HANGOVERS WENT, THIS MORNING'S wasn't so bad. I'd kept my breakfast down thus far and managed to communicate on some level with our guests before they finally vacated the premises. Dad and Emma had left soon after and with them any remaining awkwardness over last night's affairs, leaving me to collapse gratefully into a sun lounger and sleep the remainder of the morning away.

I awoke to the shrill sound of my cell, the vibrating device traveling across the metal side table with an excruciating rattle. Groaning, I flung my hand out and grabbed the beastly thing, answering the call just as I registered the number to be Unknown.

"Hello?" I croaked.

"Miss Sawyer?" came a smooth feminine tone.

"Yes."

"It's Cara, Dr Tate's secretary."

Shit! My shrink! I checked my watch. My appointment had been scheduled for ten minutes previous.

"We were just wondering if you were on your way."

"Apologies, I've been"—I coughed—"unwell this morning."

"I'm very sorry to hear that, Miss Sawyer. Dr Tate was hoping we could reschedule for later today but—"

"Later is fine," I interjected, guilt and eagerness to see him kicking in. "What time?"

"Would two-thirty suit?"

That would give me an hour to get ready and go. "Absolutely."

"Excellent, Dr Tate will be very pleased. Goodbye, Miss Sawyer."

Hanging up the call, I flopped back against the lounger. I just needed to muster the energy to move. Once I was in the sanctity of his office I could relax and let go of this pent-up emotion. He could put the hard work into making sense of my chaotic thoughts, recent discoveries and my sudden gay tendencies. I just couldn't get my head around any of it. Even in the cold light of a new day, the memory of Emma and her naked form kick-started an excitement in me that I couldn't shake.

Jumping in the shower, I turned on the jets in the hope that the water would somehow cleanse my brain and lift the post-drinking fog. I was wrong. My body reveled in the harsh onslaught of the water against my sensitized skin, still raw from the abrasive wall, and my mind flooded with images of her—her seductive smile, her teasing tongue, her body entwined with Diana and their erotic play...

I knew I didn't have the time for it but I reached for the showerhead anyway, bringing it down and instinctively navigating it to where my body craved its pleasurable force most. I inhaled sharply as it made contact with my painfully taut nipples, the relentless stream sending sparks of delight rippling through me as I envisaged Emma upon me, teasing me, coaxing me...I visualized her mouth travelling down my front as her hands pressed my thighs apart and shamelessly raised my leg to the wall, offering up my clit to the strumming beat of the water...her tongue.

My orgasm came fast and strong, the force of it sending me back against the cold wall and the showerhead dropping with a thud to the floor. It immediately sprang to life, the freed head lunging around like a live snake as it sprayed water this way and that.

"*Shit!*" I swore, my post-orgasm calm dissipating as I took in the soaked room and grabbed the blasted thing.

I was just setting it back into its holder when a banging started up on the bathroom door.

I cleared my throat to call out, but Lily's voice beat me to it. "Miss Sawyer? Are you okay?"

Bloody hell! Now I had Lily in a tizz. "Hey, Lily, all good, just dropped the bottle."

"Good, good, I was worried when I realized you were still at home, and then I heard the bang. I hope your father didn't get you so tipsy last night that you're only just moving."

I smiled. Her gentle admonishment of him was amusing and her worry for me, endearing. She really did make living under this roof much more bearable. Her, the stables, my car, and the gym, they were the things that I lived for. Or at least I used to.

"Don't worry, Lily, I'm fine."

But was I fine? I had no idea. Life had suddenly been turned on its head. It wasn't like I'd had a "normal" existence before. Certainly not the average Joe when living with a man like my stepfather. But now...

I couldn't even begin to imagine a man ever evoking the same intense reaction in me as Emma had with just a look. What did that mean? At twenty-two, was I suddenly going to change my sexuality or was it her? And only her? For the first time in a long time, I really needed that shrink appointment. The realization had me racing out of the shower and drying myself off.

Lily disappeared about her business once she was satisfied all was well and established that I would be home for dinner that night which freed me to get dressed in peace. I pulled on a simple pair of jeans and a hoody, grateful that my shrink didn't require me to maintain a superficial high-class demeanor like my stepfather, he was happy to let me be me. In fact, he preferred it that way. It "encouraged honesty" he had once told Dad after witnessing him berating me for my lack of finesse. I smiled at the memory. Since then he'd been a firm favorite in my book, my confidante, paid for or otherwise. He'd helped me through the death of my mother at the influential age of eight, protected my sanity from my overbearing stepfather and the many women he had inflicted on me over the years. Would this latest revelation surprise him? Probably not...

Clothed and ready to face the music, I jumped into my convertible Mustang, turned the music up high and blasted away any remaining cobwebs. Yes, there definitely were some things I had to be grateful to Daddy for and the powerful V8 engine beneath me was one of them. And, yes, I could leave him; he certainly deserved to be alone. But giving up my lifestyle was no easy feat and the idea was frankly terrifying.

Pulling into the basement parking lot of the exclusive office building, I shook off the uneasy thought. He wasn't really around all that much. So long as he didn't push his matchmaking schemes too far things would be okay. Stepping out of the car, I leaned across the front seat to extract my handbag—

"Abi?"

I'd know that voice anywhere. Straightening up, I spun on my heel to face its captivating owner, Emma. She oozed both sex and sophistication. Her hair pulled back in a severe ponytail accentuating her high cheekbones and enchanting green eyes. Her enviable figure, encased in a perfectly tailored gray suit and green satin blouse, was jaw-droppingly statuesque, made all the more so by another pair of stilettos, this time in the subtle shade of gray.

Finally, I stopped gawping long enough to speak. "Emma, what are you doing here?"

"Same as you I expect," she smiled, her gaze traveling the length of me, taking in my casual state of dress and making me feel self-conscious. She had the same ability as Dad, to make me feel unworthy with just a look. But with her it wasn't the way she looked at me. No, she looked genuinely delighted right now. It was how I saw her that made me feel so inadequate. She was a goddess and I...blah.

Stressing over my appearance, delayed her words sinking in—same as me?—what could she mean by that?

"I get the impression your stepfather keeps all of the women in his life on a tight leash," she added.

"You're here to see Dr Tate?"

She eyed me, her expression turning wary at my obvious confusion. "Are you not aware of anyone else having visited him?"

By anyone else, she clearly meant his previous women.

"No, should I have been?" I asked.

"No...no, of course not," she said, pasting on a smile that didn't quite meet her eyes. "I'm sorry, Abi, forget I said anything, I'll see you later."

"Emma, wait..." I reached out to catch her arm but she pulled back from the contact.

"I have to go, your stepfather is expecting me home." She flicked her eyes about her nervously and then turned and walked away.

I watched after her, frozen to the spot, completely flummoxed. What the hell was he playing at? She couldn't mean that he'd arranged for her to see Dr Tate too. A growing feeling of unease set in. The suggestion that he sent all his women here was positively worrying.

I'd always believed these appointments to be the one caring thing my stepfather had ever done for me, giving me an outlet where I could vent my frustrations, talk about my deepest fears, feel like I wasn't alone...

However, come to think of it, when had he done anything that wasn't about his own gain? Would he sink as low as to use a shrink? It would be the perfect way to keep abreast of every little thing that went on in my world. But to what end?

And what about doctor-client confidentiality? Betrayal cut through me like a knife. Dr Tate was my safety blanket, I trusted him more than anyone else 1 knew. Could he really be capable of such duplicity? But even as I thought it, I knew it was true. After all, it was amazing what someone would do when you threw enough money at them. Life with Dad had certainly taught me that.

Suddenly, I felt bereft; the warm, fuzzy feeling that normally accompanied these sessions replaced with cold apprehension. What was I to do now? I couldn't very well turn away and leave. Dad would know something was up and then I'd have to face that showdown, something I didn't want to do until I knew the real reason behind these sessions, and anything else my stepfather might be keeping from me.

Mind made up, I locked the car and headed to the office, keen not to be late. Until I established the extent of Dr Tate's involvement with my stepfather, I would simply have to watch what I said...

Chapter Six

BY THE TIME I GOT home, I was a boiling pot of rage. Each time Dr Tate probed, all I could think was that my stepfather was orchestrating the whole thing, extracting my innermost thoughts for his own perusal. I had managed to stave off giving much away, brushing over last night's dinner with some mention of Daniel, and then spent the entire drive home second-guessing Dad's intentions.

Now that I was home, I wanted nothing more than to crawl into bed with some painkillers and sleep off the dregs of my hangover, saving my troubled thoughts for tomorrow when I could hopefully think more clearly. But it wasn't to be. As soon as I opened the front door, my stepfather's raised voice reached me from the sitting room.

"It was embarrassing, Emma!"

"I didn't see anyone else complaining," came Emma's defiant response. Even from this distance I could sense she was upset, the quiver in her voice belying the strength in her words.

"You were exhausted by the time I got to have you."

Emma snorted. "With good reason."

"It's simply not good enough, I expect more from my women." His tone had taken on a threatening edge that sent my blood cold. "You were given a strict regime of exercise to ensure you had the strength and stamina to be an adequate wife, I don't appreciate you not fulfilling your side of the bargain."

"But I have done, I work hard and do exactly as your trainer asks."

I couldn't believe what I was hearing. Surely he hadn't set her up with a training regime in order to perform sexually? The idea was downright perverted.

"Then perhaps it's with him I need this discussion. Go and change. Meet me at the gym in thirty minutes, let's see if Mick can start you on a new routine this afternoon."

I could hear movement and realized they were heading my way. I ducked out of the hall and into the nearest available room, realizing too late it was Dad's study. This room was never left open, so to find myself in it was a surprise. The footsteps followed on my tail and I ducked behind the door just as my stepfather strode in, swearing under his breath.

I could hear him rustle about at his desk and then he left, pulling the door to behind him and turning his key in the lock, trapping me inside.

Fuck, now what am I to do?

Scouting about the study, I tried to think. Would he have a spare key in the room? I didn't even know where to look. I hadn't seen the inside of this room in years. But I couldn't very well just stay here and wait for him to return. Moving to the desk, I started to rifle through the drawers and then it hit me, the reason this room was always locked. Everything he wished to keep private would be stored here. It was the perfect opportunity for me to uncover what he was up to.

Leaving the desk, I headed for one of the large filing cabinets that lined the walls of the room just as the sound of a cell phone ringing started up. The flashing device caught my eye from its position on the desk. Any minute now he would be coming back to retrieve it, he never went anywhere without it. I looked longingly at the filing cabinet and decided to risk a quick glance.

Pulling out the top drawer, I scanned the overwhelming number of dividers looking for anything that might be relevant. Spotting one that bore my mother's name, I lifted it out and flicked it open. It was hefty, larger than I would have expected. It contained her death certificate, along with a copy of her will and a multitude of what looked to be financial documents and land deeds. For a woman I believed to be penniless in her own right, this made no sense. I had always been encouraged to believe my stepfather had lifted her from nothing and gifted her an amazing life. And with no living relatives to speak of, I'd never been told any different...

Extracting the will, I started to scan the pages. It didn't take long to discover the magnitude of my mother's wealth and that she had bestowed a sizable chunk of her estate to me in trust. I stared at the words before me, shock and confusion taking hold as the meaning sunk in. I was an heiress. I had money and land. I wasn't beholden to my stepfather. And he knew all this but kept it from me. Why?

The sound of hurried footsteps approaching spurred me into movement and I stuffed the file back into the cabinet, closing the drawer and positioning myself next to the doorway just as the key turned in the lock.

Adrenaline coursed through me as I watched him enter the room before me and head for his desk. I knew now was my only chance. Creeping around the door, I backed up to the entrance, my eyes never leaving him until I was safely past the threshold and I turned—

"Abi?"

Shit!

"Dad," I said spinning back to face him, a smile pasted to my lips. "I was going to chat to you about Daniel but I can tell you're busy. We can catch up later."

"Daniel you say"—he studied me intently—"sounds interesting, why don't we catch up over dinner tonight?"

"Dinner...lovely," I fumbled over my response, cursing the elevated pitch to my voice and the heat creeping into my cheeks.

"He really does seem to have made an impression."

Relief swept through me as he misinterpreted the cause of my peculiar state. "Uh-huh."

"Well, I look forward to the details tonight—see you at eight, Abi."

I nodded and spun on my heel, heading for the staircase once more, anxious to get away from him and desperate for some time to myself to make sense of my confused thoughts. There was so much I needed to find out, starting with the full extent of what my stepfather had kept from me and why. He had always been a stranger to me, but now he was someone else, something else. I feared him, but more than that was a growing sense of hatred toward him. Recounting all that I knew him guilty of made me sick to the stomach. How could he have given me such a false impression of my own mother and kept my inheritance from me? How could he send me to a shrink just to keep tabs on me? How could he treat his women like he did? Was that how he had been with my mother? What if her death...?

I rammed my fist against my mouth, a sudden surge of nausea hitting me hard as I tried to push the thought from my mind. My eyes flicked back toward the study and I watched as he locked the door and headed to the back of the house. He was no doubt on his way to the gymnasium where Emma would be waiting.

Poor girl. What was she doing with a man like him? She couldn't possibly love him and yet, was she that callous to be with him for the money? From the time I had spent with her, I couldn't believe it to be true. I just didn't understand it. And I wanted to understand it. I wanted to understand her. And suddenly I wanted to see her...badly. Her motives were suspicious at best, but I didn't care right now, I just wanted the pain of all this information taken away and replaced with the passion she inspired in me.

I knew I had a couple of hours to kill before I could seek her out so I continued to my room, my mind racing with unanswered questions and half-baked plans of what I could do next.

An hour and a half later, with no clear answers or strategy in place, I headed for the gym, unable to wait any longer. I had changed into a baby pink crop top and low-slung training pants under the pretense of heading for a session myself.

I found Emma still mid-workout. Dad had really meant it when he said she would be worked harder. She sat at the weights machine, doing a pec fly. Her muscles hard through exertion, a sheen of perspiration covering her exposed skin. Did Dad choose her clothing too? Her skimpy hot pants clung to her like a second skin. Her exercise bra, despite the lack of material, was doing an adequate job of keeping her ample breasts in check but her nipples protruded through the soft fabric, begging to be gawped at. Each time she pulled back, it stretched captivatingly tight against her.

"Quite a sight, isn't she?"

I spun on my heel toward the voice. It was Mick, the personal trainer, and he had caught me blatantly ogling.

Heat crept into my cheeks as I struggled to say something.

"Don't worry, I won't give you away," he said playfully. "Why don't you come and join us? Emma's coming to the end of her regime anyway."

At the word "regime" and the reminder of what it had meant for my stepfather, the color deepened in my cheeks, but I stood my ground.

"That would be great," I said. "So long as I'm not in the way, I hadn't realized Emma would still be here."

He didn't believe me for a second. "I'm sure she won't mind, she's probably bored of having to work with just me and this score card, perhaps a bit of competition will help boost things a little."

"Competition?" I said tentatively as I followed him into the room.

Spotting our approach, Emma halted her repetitions and sent me a dazzling smile. I fought hard to keep my eyes on her face but they were constantly drawn to her chest and those two taut peaks...

"Abi wants to put some time in, so I thought we could have a bit of a wager between the two of you, spice things up a little?"

Emma took up her towel and started to rub away the perspiration, all the while her eyes flicking back to mine, catching me looking where I shouldn't.

She let out a small giggle. "A wager, you say?"

"Aye, how about the one who can push the most weight with the same repetitions can treat the other to something of their choosing?" He winked at me as he said it and I wondered what he was implying, my mind following a path of possibilities that really wasn't helping me stay focused in the moment.

"Sure," she said, throwing her towel down and looking to me. "You should get warmed up first though, don't want you getting yourself an injury."

And that was all the encouragement I needed. I never tackled weights until after my run and I decided not to change the habit. I wanted to impress her with what I was capable of. She was clearly happy enough to wait for me and Mick was enjoying the banter.

A short run, a stint on the rowing machine and I was warmed up and ready for her...or rather our wager. Every time I had glanced in her direction, her eyes had been on me, watching me, her thoughts unreadable but the smile that touched her lips was more than just friendly. I was sure of it.

"Right then, ladies, I figure we'll go for the best of seven moves that test you top to bottom starting with the upper body..."

Obediently, we did as instructed. Each taking our turn while the other watched. Some moves more torturous than others, not to carry out but to observe. Watching her work out was like foreplay without the contact. Her body captivated me. And as things heated up, it became more and more obvious that she found me just as appealing.

"Right, you're level pegging, ladies. It's going to come down to the thigh abductors in the final showdown, so to speak!" Mick was doing a good job of ignoring our blatant appreciation of one another. Either that or it was simply that we weren't really aware of him, save for his next instruction. "Off you go, Abi."

Settling back into the machine, Mick adjusted the weights and I began my reps, aware that they were both watching intently, their eyes focusing at the juncture between my thighs as I pushed the cushioned plates apart. Their obvious appreciation of what they saw sent ripples of excitement running through me and the familiar ache sparked between my legs. I lost count of where I was, my mind focusing solely on their enjoyment of me. The sudden image of the three of us entwined filled my mind and heat soared to my cheeks, my legs faltering mid-rep.

"Hey, easy tiger, this set should be a breeze for you," Mick teased, his eyes shooting to my face. "You wanting to call it a day?"

"No way," I said, my competitive spirit kicking in, I released the weight and rubbed at my nose. "Just thought I was going to sneeze."

I caught Emma smiling at me in obvious amusement.

"What's so funny?" I asked, the tension in my body from the workout and direction of my thoughts adding heat to my voice.

"Sorry, I didn't mean to offend you," she hurried out. "You just looked adorable when you did that thing with your nose."

Mick rolled his eyes. "Never mind adorable, Emma, this is supposed to be a competition and it's your turn."

The redness in my cheeks deepened. Adorable wasn't how I wanted her to see me right now, especially when I was so convinced her intentions were far from sweet and innocent not seconds before. Rubbing myself down, I moved out of the way of the machine and watched as she took my place.

It was clear from Emma's very first rep why I'd elicited the reaction I had. As her legs spread wide it was my turn to be captivated by the provocative move, my eyes taking in their fill of the open stance, my hands itching to cup her inner thighs as they drew apart...

An incessant beeping started up from the direction of Mick and glancing across I saw him play with his watch, cutting off the sound.

"Apologies, ladies, but I have to give a status report to Mr. Sawyer, he's keen to see how Emma has performed."

At the mention of my stepfather, Emma released the weight with a thud and grimaced.

"Hey, don't look so glum!" he hurried out. "I will be very complimentary, don't you worry."

Emma gave him a genuine smile. "Thank you."

"Let me know who wins, won't you?" he added with a wink before turning to leave.

I just stared after his retreating form, incapable of speech, my chest rising and falling in almost pant-like gasps as the realization that we were about to be alone, well and truly alone, hit home.

Chapter Seven

As THE DOOR CLOSED BEHIND Mick, an awkward silence cut through the charged atmosphere. I no longer knew where to look. Mick's presence had somehow made it okay to enjoy one another, safe in the knowledge that nothing could happen, but now he was gone...

"I believe it's your turn," Emma said, rescuing me from my nerves. She unfolded her glistening form from the seat and gestured for me to take her place.

I did so willingly, desperate to busy myself once more. As I positioned my thighs at the pads, she bent forward to up the weight for me. Her body was so close that her hair fell forward to brush across my shoulder, her delicious scent drawing me in. I had to force myself not to turn to her. To try and remember who she was. To tell myself, my mind was playing tricks on me. That this couldn't possibly be happening. That this could *never* happen.

"All set," she said, sending me a heated look that shattered my misgivings in one fell swoop.

Mutely, I nodded. I could do this, I could keep control. I could push this weight in my sleep...and ignore the crazy ache in my belly...Honest...

As my thighs moved outward, Emma's brazen gaze followed. Two reps in and I watched her imprison her bottom lip between her teeth, my own mouth helplessly mimicking...four reps in, she started rubbing at her throat, her fingers working into the sensitive skin in a seemingly subconscious fashion. As I moved into the widest point of rep five, she inhaled sharply, her bare abs flexing with the move.

"You have an amazing body, Abi."

Her breathless words sent my thighs collapsing inward, the weight clashing back to rest as blood rushed to service the tantalizing ache that had increased tenfold with her words. Their utterance serving to confirm everything that until then had been potential imaginings in my mind.

"Sorry," she blurted. "I hadn't meant to startle you."

"You didn't," I said, forgetting the machine at my thighs and any sense of what was right as I looked up at her, trying to show her just how much I appreciated her back. Just how much I wanted her too. If only she would make the first move...

"Please continue," she said, gesturing to my legs, her eyes flashing with a sexual hunger that I knew would be mirrored in my own. I did as she instructed, nursing my body as I went, clenching my thighs as tight as I could when the machine permitted, allowing my body to build a tension of an entirely different form to the one intended by the workout.

My nipples started to strain against the fabric of my bra, their sensitized peaks hungry for attention. My pulsing clit worked with the friction of the tight-fitting gym pants to coax and tease the growing fire in my veins. And then, to my salacious delight, she stepped forward.

"May I?" she asked, looking to my thighs. "I'd like to feel you as you move."

I swallowed hard and nodded. *God, yes!* my mind screamed.

Slowly, she dropped to her knees before me, her tongue flicking out to moisten her lips. The gesture so carnal that I faltered mid-rep and she tutted, shaking her head playfully at my lapse in form. And then her hands were at my knees, her touch teasingly soft. She nodded at me and I knew she wanted me to move once more, but my focus was very much on the feel of her against me, my concentration and strength to push the weight lost. But she didn't budge. Her message was clear. Until I moved, she wasn't going to either.

Closing my eyes, I tilted my head back and fought against the weight, spreading my thighs apart and languishing in my reward as her hands slid inwards, her palms molding to my inner thighs.

"You're so strong," she said in fascination as her hands began an upward caress, her stroke tormentingly light and rising further with each completed rep.

Please, God, please! I internally begged. I needed her touch upon me, right at the source of my ache, not teasingly close...

I started to delay the midpoint of my rep, anything to keep my legs spread so that she could reach the access I craved. Finally, she brushed across me. The move so painfully brief I wondered if I'd imagined it. I wanted to openly beg her, but my inexperience wouldn't let me. Instead, I squirmed in the seat, my concentration well and truly off the weight at my thighs as my body caved in to the pressure, my legs falling inward on a tormented moan.

"Aw, baby, is it too hard?"

My eyes flew open at her words. Gone was happy Emma from yesterday's horse ride.

Sexy, totally wanton, and fuckable Emma from last night was before me now.

"Spread them for me," she demanded.

I moaned and pressed against the weight as she asked, her palms now massaging hungrily into my thighs.

"Come on, you can do this, baby," she encouraged, her fingers never ceasing in their upward exploration, her eyes watching over me, hot and hungry.

Under the spell of her look, I forgot the pain of the weight and continued to complete the reps, my mind solely occupied by the effect of her blazing green eyes, the touch of her feminine fingers, and the feel of her soft, round breasts as they brushed against my knees.

"I reckon you have four more to go, else I win," she said softly.

Four? I wasn't even sure that was right, but in all honesty, I no longer knew which way was up or how to count!

She was pushing me to the edge and she knew it. Spreading my thighs again, I moaned in delight as she finally made contact with my throbbing clit, this time the touch undeniable as the soft pads of her thumbs began to rotate over me in an orgasm-inducing tempo. Immediately, I stiffened, forcing my legs to work against the opposing weight and remain wide as I pleaded her with my body to not stop. I could feel my climax swiftly coming, the rigidity of my working muscles serving to add to the deliciously-rising tension. But as my orgasm neared, my strength to hold the weight wore out and I was forced to surrender to it, my legs coming together on an agonizing moan.

To hell with the fucking wager!

Thrusting my legs out of the trappings of the machine, I spread myself before her, making it clear I didn't want her to stop.

"You give up?" she teased, but she didn't deny me, her expert fingers returning to take up the same tempo over me, all the while her heated gaze drinking in my wanton state. I thrust my lower body up as my legs gripped the machine beneath me, the divine tension quick to take over me once more. And then I shattered before her, the intensity of my orgasm like nothing I had ever experienced at the hands of another.

But I was quick to recover. Humiliation giving me a rude awakening as I realized just how quick I'd been to come. God, she would think me so inexperienced. Or easy. Or both. I wasn't sure which was worse. Chancing a glance at her, I needn't have worried. Her eyes were ablaze with need. Whatever she thought of me, she wanted me with the same intense need that had possessed me not minutes before.

"I believe I win, Abi."

"Probably," I conceded, an element of shyness creeping into my voice in the aftermath of my orgasm.

"So I get to choose my prize?"

I nodded, sexual excitement bubbling anew as I got an inkling of where this was heading.

"I'd like to see you naked."

What! I hadn't expected that. Not so directly at any rate.

"Please, Abi, your body captivates me. I want to see it."

She moved back to allow me space to stand and, swallowing back my nerves, I stood.

What did it matter anyhow? She clearly liked what she had seen so far. Chances were she would like me even more when I removed my clothes...I hoped.

Stepping out of my trainers, I discarded my socks and shimmied off my training pants, my confidence growing as with each item her eyes darkened, her pupils dilating with her mounting desire. And then, as I reached behind my back to take hold of the bra clasp, I spied her breathing still and I knew I had her one hundred percent under my spell. I was doing this to her. *Me!*

A smile formed at my lips.

"Please," she said, her voice almost a whisper now, her eyes burning into my chest as she waited for the fabric to drop.

"Your wish is my command," I said, my lust-filled voice sounding foreign to my own ears.

Letting the bra slip to the floor, the cool air of the gym swept across my front, teasing my exposed nipples to tautened peaks once more, the thrilling sensation reigniting the warmth in my core.

Before me, Emma exhaled slowly, the appreciation in her gaze almost too much to believe.

"You are beautiful," she whispered, stepping forward and reaching out to brush my hair back over my shoulders, her eyes scanning every last bit of me. "Tell me, have you ever been with a woman before me?"

I shook my head. I couldn't speak. I couldn't breathe. Fear that it would break the moment rendering me still.

She smiled. "So I'm your first..."

Her voice trailed off as she lowered her gaze, her eyes following her hands as she traced an exploratory path along my upper body, encircling each aching mound with teasing proximity, her caress getting ever closer but not quite upon the hardened peaks. The move agonizing, yet totally erotic.

"You see, the benefit of being with a woman is that we know what the other likes, we know just how to tease"—a hand brushed over the surface of one nipple and I gasped at the ricocheting shoot of pleasure—"we know just how to create such a burning within that it's not just the act of coming that consumes you, but the whole process of getting there."

Her mouth was so close to mine, I only had to tilt forward and I would be able to taste her, but still I didn't dare...

"And since you are to be my slave..."

My eyes shot to hers. "Slave?"

"Oh, yes," she said playfully. "I want my prize to be you as my slave, doing exactly as I ask, do you object?"

She knew she needn't have asked, I was practically salivating at the thought as my whole body begged to be at this woman's beck and call.

"No," I whispered.

"Good," she said, stepping back from me. "The next thing you can do is remove my clothing. That workout has left me rather hot and bothered."

I could scarcely breathe for the thrill of it. I'd wanted to do this from the first moment I'd seen her: to undress her, to touch her, to have the freedom to enjoy her. And now she was commanding me to do it.

Tentatively, I raised my hands to her shoulders and hooked my fingers beneath her bra straps, reveling in the feel of her soft warm skin beneath them as, slowly, I stroked outward, forcing the straps down over her arms until the fabric resisted the move.

Mouth dry with anticipation, I left the straps and moved my hands inward to the top of each mound and with bated breath I slipped them beneath the taut fabric, savoring every bit of her soft, full flesh and then the sudden hardness of her pert nipples as they pressed into my palm. She moaned at the contact and I bit my lip against the surge of excitement rushing through me, the experience so new and intensely erotic.

Lifting her breasts from the restraint of the cups, I dropped my eyes to enjoy the sight of their now prominent position above the bunched up fabric. She was stunning. I couldn't imagine ever getting enough of her. I watched my hands move over her, riveted by the sight, the feel and the effect I was having on her. I was desperate to grope her hard, to pinch at her nipples, to toy with her...and then her words filled my mind...

Women know just how to tease.

I would know just how to tease.

With growing confidence, I let my instincts take over. Filling my palms with the soft, pliable flesh once more, I imprisoned their stiffened peaks between my thumb and forefinger, rolling them teasingly. The move milked sounds from her delectable throat that had me going wild with need and upping the ferocity of my caress. I crushed her lips with my own, my tongue joining hers in a fierce mating battle. The feel of her delicate, feminine tongue against my own, so different and so thrilling, had a fire coursing through me.

Desperate to taste every last bit of her, I worked her back against the weight machine, removing her bra as I went. Forcing her to sit, I tore my mouth from her own to trace a path along her neck, savoring her delicious saltiness as I went.

She was whimpering above me, one hand gripping at the machine, the other thrust into my hair. The experience so all-consuming, I never wanted it to end.

As I reached the peak of one pert nipple, I let my tongue trace around it, enjoying the dimpled flesh beneath, and then I flicked across the tip, loving how it made her buck for me. I did it again, repeatedly, and she began to squirm in the seat. I took up the other nipple with my hand, groping the swollen flesh with a mounting ferocity that mirrored the climbing madness inside.

"More, Abi, I need more!"

I smiled at her words, my mouth moving over the nipple to suck the entirety into the cavern of my mouth. She almost knocked me to the floor as her body undulated with the move and I pressed against her, holding her steady as both my hand and mouth continued to work her, the feel of her damp, hot pants as she started to rock against my torso driving me on.

Then I remembered how it felt to have her hands pressing against my thighs earlier and I did exactly that. Forcing her legs further apart, I held her spread and away from me, teasing her with the lack of contact on her eager clit while my mouth and hands continued to devour her breasts.

"Oh, Fuck! Abi! Please!"

Control consumed me, it's effect dizzying and intoxicating, she was mine...

"What is it, baby?" I said, giving her a hint of my lower body against her pussy.

She threw her head back and bucked her crotch toward me, trying to maintain the contact. I smiled at her desperation, getting high on the need I had aroused in her. Slowly, I allowed my hands to travel up her thighs, loving how her whole body tensed at the move. I stopped at either side of her crotch, my fingers massaging into her skin, teasing her just as she had me.

She moaned and flung her hands outward, grasping at the frame of the machine as she writhed to direct my fingers where she wanted them.

"Patience, baby, I need you naked first."

Obediently she stilled and, bringing her legs together, I pulled off her bottoms, tossing them to the side. My hands were quick to return, my eagerness to have her spread naked before me taking over as I shoved her thighs apart once more. She didn't stop me. Her lack of resistance only serving to heighten my out of control desire as I realized she would permit me anything.

My eyes dropped to her pussy, the neatly trimmed area dripping in excitement. Fascinated, I slipped my fingers between her folds, savoring the feel of her, so different from me and yet the same. Her body reared against the touch, her clit pulsing beneath my palm as I traveled lower to dip my fingers inside her, surrounding them with her warm, wet center and coating myself with her hot juices before withdrawing to stroke at her throbbing clit.

She cried out and her eyes flung to mine. I repeated the move, holding her gaze intently, getting off on the erotic pleasure I saw there. Then I brought my fingers to my mouth and slid them in, sucking them clean. She moaned at the sight, her lips parting with the sound.

Dipping my fingers within her again, I coated them thoroughly, realizing I could never get enough of just feeling her in this way. Bringing my fingers back up, I moved them before her open mouth, teasing them before her lips.

"You want some, baby?"

Her eyes dropped to my slick fingers and, hungrily, she moved her mouth over them. A groan escaped my lips as she sucked at them, her tongue eagerly working them clean.

"You are such a dirty bitch." I don't know where the words came from but I was fascinated by her and out of control. My eyes shot to hers to see if I had offended her but they were ablaze with need.

"More," she cried.

Obediently I lowered my hand, she was so wet and ready that I moved all four fingers within her, letting my thumb caress her clit.

She moaned, her body picking up its rhythm against me, I realized her climax was building, I could see the muscles working in her legs, the color rising in her cheeks...not yet...

"Easy, baby, easy."

I withdrew my hand and raised it once more to her lips, watching in wonder as she took all four fingers into her mouth, closing her lips around them, all the while her eyes fixed on mine.

Horny as fuck, I tore my hand away and crushed my lips over hers, kissing her hard, savoring the taste of her pussy in her mouth. I wanted more. I wasn't ready for this to end. Not yet, I wanted to experience all of her.

Tearing my mouth from hers, I traveled down her wildly pulsing throat, down the valley between her breasts...

Spying my intent, she flung her hands to my hair and encouraged me down.

"Patience," I said taking her hands and repositioning them at the frame, loving how open it left her, how it thrust her breasts forward. Cupping each mound, I flicked my tongue over them in turn, wetting each peak before moving to trace a path down her torso, dipping into her belly button and then onward to her delicious cunt.

With my hands pressing her thighs apart, I probed the area, my tongue flicking over her clit—

"God, yes!" she screamed, jerking against me, her crotch riding my face.

I repeated the move, my tongue working her as she built up her tempo against me. She hooked her feet between my legs, encouraging me to move against her. My body reveled in the contact, quickly picking up a rhythm of its own as the need for release swept through me. Our moans echoed around the gymnasium, drowning out the world outside, our focus entirely on each other.

She shattered about me in what felt like seconds, her body convulsing wildly. Clamping my thighs shut around her feet I swiftly followed, the intensity of her orgasm fueling my own. Crying out, I fell against her, my head dropping to her warm, inviting thigh as I enjoyed the spasms that racked my body and the feeling of contentment that soon followed.

I have no idea how long we stayed like that, but neither of us seemed inclined to move. Our bodies now sated and relaxed felt right together. Her fingers moved through my hair, toying with the strands and she sighed contentedly. The sound brought a smile to my lips. No matter how wrong it was, what we had just shared felt one hundred percent right.

And then the mood changed. Her hand froze at my head, her body tensing beneath me. My eyes snapped to hers and I could see she was looking at the doorway behind me, her face horror-stricken.

Please don't be Dad! was the plea going through my mind as I straightened to look over my shoulder.

Relief washed over me, quickly followed by shame. Mick was lounging in the open doorway, his eyes drinking in the view.

"Err, hi," I said sheepishly.

"Hi, yourselves," he drawled, his body unmoving. "Do you know what torture it is to witness that and not come anywhere near the pair of you? If your Dad—"

"Mick!" My worried gaze turned to Emma, her form unmoving as she continued to watch him with a growing sense of panic. It was clear it was more than simply embarrassment. She looked terrified. And it wouldn't be Mick she was scared of. It was my stepfather.

"It's okay, Emma," I assured her, my body shielding her from Mick's view as she lifted her eyes to mine, clearly struggling to believe me.

"Mick won't say a word"—I fixed him with a pointed stare—"will you?"

"Hell no! Do you know what he would do to me if he even knew I'd seen you both?"

"See, Emma, it's going to be fine," I stressed as I turned to face her once more. "No one else need know, okay?"

She relaxed slightly before me and nodded.

"I hate to break this up, ladies, but I believe you're expected at dinner in half an hour."

"Christ, is it that time already?" I flicked my gaze to my watch. He was right, we needed to get dressed and get out of there. Throwing him a look over my shoulder, I said sarcastically, "Would you mind giving us some privacy then?"

"Spoilsport," he teased, his eyes flashing as he pushed himself off the doorframe and turned away. "I'll be back in five, ladies, trust you will be gone by then."

Chapter Eight

Forty-five minutes later, showered and wearing a full-length dress that Dad would approve of, I entered the dining room. Emma and Dad were already tucking into dinner. Emma looked up from her plate to send me a heart-warming smile, her cheeks flushing beneath her makeup and I knew her thoughts were on the events of the afternoon, just as mine were.

"Good evening," I said, returning her smile with surprising ease considering Dad's brooding presence at the head of the table.

"So you finally decided to join us?" he snapped, his glowering gaze burning into me as I took up the empty seat opposite Emma.

I forced myself to look right at him, my smile still fixed to my face. "I'm sor—"

"Save it!" he said, putting an end to my apology. Not that it really mattered; I didn't mean it anyway. "If it wasn't for my intrigue at our conversation over Daniel earlier I'd send you elsewhere to eat."

Shit! I had totally forgotten about my suggestive words regarding

Daniel. I really didn't want to have *that* talk now, especially in front of Emma.

"Sorry, Daddy," I tried again, doing my best to look contrite.

"Well, I assume you must have good reason?" he said, taking up his cutlery, his focus returning to the food before him.

The best, I thought, as an image of Emma shattering above me filled my mind and sent my cheeks flaming. I needed to get a grip and clawing onto the first excuse I could think of, said, "I had a phone call."

His eyes flicked back to mine, their depths glittering with ignited excitement, his forked food pausing mid-air. "Daniel, perhaps?"

"Yes," I blurted before I could think better of it, desperation to be out of his bad books winning out.

"Well, I'll be damned!" he smiled. "I just knew he'd take a liking to you"—his attention turned to Emma—"it's like I said, keeping her around really does have its benefits."

His heartless words left his mouth so easily, and as soon as they were out his eyes returned to his plate, his mind obviously thinking on his grand master plan. He wasn't even waiting on Emma for a response. And it certainly didn't warrant one from me. I eyed her over the table, trying to gauge her reaction. I didn't need to try hard. Her eyes glistened in the light as they held my gaze, the color in her cheeks now non-existent.

The strong urge to cover her hand with my own, to reassure her that she needn't be upset on my behalf, forced me to look away and I tried to turn my attention to eating. Yet I could sense she still watched me, her body motionless, her knuckles white around the stem of her wine glass.

I chanced a glance, my gaze imploring as I looked from her face to her food in a silent prompt for her to eat and to drop whatever thought was running through her mind.

Slowly, she brought the wine glass to her lips and took a contemplative sip, her gaze still level with mine. But as she returned the drink to the table, her color heightened anew, a surprising warmth filling her features as she turned to look at my stepfather. "Why, yes, darling, I do believe you are incredibly lucky to have someone as special as her around."

The open adoration in her tone had my heart thudding in my chest, and a heat spreading in my lower belly. Did she not realize how she sounded?

Her obvious affection hadn't gone unnoticed by my stepfather either, his eyes narrowing on his fiancée. "So you've noticed her qualities too?"

My eyes shot to hers once more, the warning in them clear: Don't go there! Even just a hint and it's game over. There was no telling what he would do...

"Oh, yes, I can see *exactly* why you would keep her around."

I couldn't breathe, fear and some unidentifiable emotion rendering me immobile. I fixed my gaze on my plate, my hands working the cutlery unseeingly over the food.

Please drop this...please drop this...please drop this!

I could feel Dad's gaze flicking between us, could almost hear the cogs in his brain working overtime as my own guilty conscience had him putting two and two together.

I needed to distract him. I needed to get the focus off me...*off us!* I was angry at Emma for her open appreciation, it was brazen and downright dangerous. But my own foolish ego couldn't help feeling boosted. My heart swelling at her defense of me.

Thankful for my well-rehearsed ability to talk bullshit where my stepfather was concerned, I looked across at him and delivered the perfect line, "Yes, well, believe me, it cuts both ways." I placed my hand on his forearm for added effect. "I am, after all, incredibly lucky to be here."

"Too right," came my father's righteous response, his arm shrugging off my contact as he took up his own drink. "And now you are about to make that decision really pay off, my girl! Daniel's father has already been in touch this morning to request we get together a week on Saturday."

Emma's eyes darted across at him. "Saturday?"

"Yes," he said, taking an appreciative swig of wine, unaware that his words had been less than favorably received. "I believe the man is very much taken with how we do things around here and is after a repeat affair."

A repeat affair? Just how much of a repeat?

A chill ran through me as I contemplated it. As much as the scene had enthralled me, as much as Daniel had filled a void, it was another thing entirely to go through it again. Not now. Not with all that I had learned that day, all the questions that remained unanswered and the undeniable attraction between Emma and I. My eyes locked with hers across the table, the idea of seeing her with another twisting my stomach and leaving me cold. She looked far from happy at the prospect too. Was she thinking the same?

"Of course, I have accepted on our behalf," he continued.

"You have?" Emma said quietly, her eyes remaining level with mine.

"Absolutely! I'm not hanging around to give him chance to cool off," he said. "Roger has suggested we spend the weekend at their lodge in the lakes. He says it's a remote, quiet area, perfect for some more private gatherings..."

His voice carried on; he was oblivious to the tension in the air, of the unsaid words passing between Emma and I. A week on Saturday, that was no time in the future. There were things I needed to get straight in my head, things that I needed to understand.

"...so what do you think?"

My stepfather turned to me, the expectant expression on his face making it clear that he was waiting on me to respond. Only one problem—I had no idea to what he was referring, not specifically at any rate and I braced myself as I posed the ignorant question, "About what?"

"Christ, Abi!"

His exclamation made me jump, and Emma visibly winced.

"Can't you stay focused for more than a second?" he admonished, his wine glass hitting the table with a resounding clunk, the red liquid sloshing to soil the crisp, white tablecloth beneath. I watched the stain seep outward, its spreading mass a fascinating reflection of my growing internal guilt and humility. "I was talking about Daniel's feelings toward you, you must have an idea as to whether he is interested? I assume he is, considering he spent the night in your room?"

Emma coughed in obvious surprise and I felt my cheeks burn. It hadn't occurred to me that this would be news to her. The realization that it was and the damning effect it would have on her opinion of me had my ears ringing. I didn't want her to think less of me. And I certainly didn't want her discovering like this.

There was nothing I could say, especially in front of my stepfather, that would make the news any easier to bear. But if I was being honest with myself, what could I possibly have to say that would get me out of this. Not when, for all my father's digging, it was me that had jumped right in and allowed things to go as far as they had.

"Well, yeah...sure, I think he likes me," I fumbled over the words and shifted uncomfortably in my seat. I watched Emma intently, desperate to catch her eye once more, but she wouldn't even look at me now, her eyes skirting anywhere but, a bad sign of her changing opinion, of that I was certain.

"Good, good," he nodded. "And what do you say, Emma? They make a great couple, don't they?"

Under the watchful gaze of my stepfather, Emma finally looked to me and raised her glass to her cherry red lips. As she tilted it to take a sip, she held my eyes hostage, her gaze steady and assessing. I couldn't breathe for fear of what she would say, of the potential disdain I would hear in her voice...

And then she blinked, her focus turning to my stepfather, a small smile touching her lips as she spoke, "Aye, they most definitely do darling."

Her words and the silky smooth tone in which she uttered them sent a chill running through me.

Did she think me a whore now? A girl that would do anything for an easy life? Had she lost all respect for me? And could I really blame her if she had?

But hang on, it wasn't like she faired any better! Not when she was marrying a man like him. And if we were being honest, wasn't it her that had *seduced* me? I could feel the anger bubbling in my belly as I tried to focus on my stepfather's continued prattle.

"Yes, I believe his father is very happy," he was saying, once more wrapped up in his own thoughts and self-congratulation. "The night's events must have really got him hooked, hence his eagerness to get together so soon. That being said"—he sent Emma a look—"some of us could have performed a little better."

Emma gave a sharp intake of breath. And I realized with horror that he was referring to her stamina, or his perceived lack thereof.

What a prick!

I grabbed the bottle and poured myself some wine, desperate to pretend I was unaware of the meaning behind his words and in dire need of the alcohol to douse the anger simmering too close to the surface. The awkward silence that descended would have had any normal person on edge. Dad, however, was utterly oblivious. Or if he was aware, he just didn't care. Yes, *didn't care*, that was much more likely.

A gentle rap on the door filled the room and both Emma and I started.

"Lord, you're both jumpy tonight," he remarked derisively, his attention turning to the doorway. "Come!"

Tom, one of Dad's burly "thugs", as I nicknamed them, entered. He was broad-shouldered and six foot four, at least; a terrifying presence of a man, but he appeared immediately humble as he nodded his respect and approached.

Ducking his head, he spoke discretely in my stepfather's ear, his voice low enough to prevent us overhearing what was being said. With a growing sense of unease, I watched as Dad's eyes flitted between us, his expression unreadable.

Seconds ticked by and yet it felt like minutes. Eventually, he straightened and my stepfather pushed his seat back, to rise with him.

"If you'll excuse me, there is something I need to tend to," he said, tossing his napkin to the table.

"But you're not finished."

I could hear the elevation to Emma's tone, could sense her rising panic like my own.

"I can cope without the extra baggage"—he reached out to take hold of Emma's chin, tilting her face up to him and turning it appraisingly side to side as though he were evaluating a piece of livestock—"and let's be honest dear, you should probably stop eating soon too. From what I hear, your body fat percentage is teetering into the unacceptable."

Emma's composure blew me away; she didn't even flinch at his words. She simply lowered her gaze and nodded into his hold, her hands placing her cutlery together on her plate.

"Good girl," he said, releasing her chin and brushing his thumb across her lips, the only sign of affection in his otherwise twisted farewell before he walked away.

I stared after his vacating form in amazement. How could he continue to surprise me with his malice? Was I really so naive as to think him redeemable on any level these days? And what of the woman in front of me? Who was she really? Underneath it all? Could she really possess a good streak if she was happy to be married to *that*?

But, frankly, who was I to judge? It wasn't like I had been running for the hills or like I was an innocent bystander in recent events.

My gaze succumbed to the magnetic pull of the womanly perfection before me and I drank her in anew. Each time our eyes connected, my body reacted, its inability to be doused by the risk of discovery was unsettling and downright terrifying in itself. There was so much I wanted to say to her, I just didn't know where to begin. I wanted to understand her, get to the bottom of why she was here, why she would be with a man like him, why she would be interested in me, of all people? I wanted to explain my own actions, what had happened with Daniel, why it had happened. It was all there, racing away in my mind and I started to speak. "Emma—"

She raised her palm to silence me, tears filling her eyes and crushing me.

"If you'll excuse me, Abi, I am quite tired..."

"P-p-please," I tried, my voice breaking. "We should talk."

"I think we have done enough today," she said, pushing herself up from the table and turning to leave.

"Please, Emma..." I could hear the desperation in my voice, but I just didn't get it. How come she could be so composed with *him* and the complete opposite with me, surely she at least owed me some of her time. "We really need to talk, to understand one..."

She looked back at me over her shoulder, her pained expression bringing an end to my words. "Not tonight," she bit out and then she turned and walked away.

I wasn't even worthy of a backward glance.

I felt sick and helpless. In forty-eight hours, my life as I knew it had been tipped on its head and I could do nothing to correct it, nothing to get it back to the way it was before...before I had met her...

And would I really want to? Hadn't I just been going through the motions of life before in blissful ignorance: doing my stepfather's bidding, fooling around with the odd guy, finding solace with a therapist whose intentions were now questionable at best.

No, I absolutely would not want to go back.

But where did that leave me? And what would I do if Dad were to find out? *What if he already had?*

The uneasy feeling that Tom had brought him news of us still gnawed at me, but I had to find time to be alone with her, we had to talk. There was something special between us, there just had to be.

Chapter Nine

THIRTY MINUTES LATER, STILL SAT alone and with a plate full of food, my conviction was wearing thin.

I kept turning it all over in my mind, the realization that each time she had shown genuine pain, I had been at the heart of it. Like when my stepfather had ridiculed me, when he had belittled me, and when he had asked me to dance to his tune in aid of his business plans. But most of all, when he had made it clear that Daniel and I had spent the night together, that had really got to her.

And what of that?

Was it the pain of jealousy? Or was it the realization that I wasn't who she thought me to be and she regretted what we had shared?

And why the hell did I care so much? Why did I want to risk my heart to someone who was as morally suspect as she?

I grimaced and shoved the plate away. I was going round in circles, getting nowhere.

The movement of the door opening made my heart skip—*Emma?*

My eyes shot eagerly to the doorway, only to find Lily stepping in. The surge of disappointment would have floored me if not for my chair.

"Sorry, Miss Sawyer, I was coming to clear the plates away. I didn't think anyone was still eating."

"We're not," I said, pushing back from the table and offering her a small smile that I knew didn't reach my eyes. "Please carry on, I'm going to call it a night anyway."

Before Lily's perceptive nature forced an interrogation I didn't feel strong enough to evade, I fled the room. I had just started to climb the stairs when Dad's study door opened and out came Tom with Mick close behind.

My gut lurched. There really was only one reason Dad would be speaking to Mick at this time of night.

I caught Mick's eye only to have him look immediately away, his avoidance even more telling than the grim expression he bore.

Hands trembling, I reached out for the balustrade and started up the stairs once more.

"Abigail."

My foot faltered over the step, my stepfather's drawn out delivery of my name turning my blood to ice.

I swallowed and paused to look at him over my shoulder. He stood in the study entrance, his face hard like granite, hands fisted at his sides.

"Daddy?"

My voice sounded so small, I couldn't tell if he'd actually heard it, not that it mattered, he knew he had my attention.

"Come here," he commanded, stepping aside so that his body now flanked the doorway, showing me in no uncertain terms that I was to join him in the study.

My stomach twisted with fear. "I'm tired, can it wait until tomorrow?" I tried, desperation to flee overwhelming any sense of obedience.

"No, Abi." His eyes shot me down. "This will not wait."

I gave the upper floor a fleeting covetous glance before turning on Jello-like legs and descending the staircase.

There was no choice, really. If I didn't come willingly, I had no doubt he would drag me there.

"Good to see there is some respect left in you," he barked as I passed.

I had to clamp my jaw shut to stop the trembling in my body giving way to the chattering of my teeth. His rage permeated off him, coming through in waves with each seething breath he took.

Fear kept my eyes fixed ahead as I walked slowly into the room, not halting until my legs pressed up against the edge of his desk. Behind me I heard the door close, followed by the sickening click of the lock and then the steady clip of his heel as he approached.

Still I couldn't look back at him.

He didn't speak until he came up alongside me. "You must think me a fool, dear child," he said, his tone menacingly low as he leaned across me to toss his cell to the desk, his body brushing mine, his unmistakable cologne filling my flared nostrils as I struggled for air.

I tried to speak but as soon as my jaw slackened, my teeth vibrated. I had seen him this mad before, of course I had, and on the occasions it had been directed at me, the result had left me unable to sit for a week.

I knew now was going to be no different.

"Nothing to say?" he asked, eying me over his hands as he worked to unbutton the cuff on one shirtsleeve, then the other.

My body swayed with my oxygen-starved brain and I reached for the stability of the desk, my nails biting painfully into the wooden surface.

"Nothing at all?" He gave a short derisive laugh. "Really, the least you could bloody well do is look at me when I address you!"

His words forced my eyes to his, and I had to swallow the squirming sound that worked its way up my throat. To whimper would only incite further malice from him, of that I had no doubt.

"Better," he said with genuine satisfaction, his eyes holding mine momentarily before breaking off to tend to the meticulous folding back of his shirtsleeves. I watched his hands as they overlapped the cloth in neat, uniform sections, not stopping until both sleeves fell the exact same distance down his arms, resting a cuff's breadth below the elbow. It was a step I had come to recognize well.

"Now let me explain something to you, child," he said, starting to pace to the left of me, his eyes flicking between me and the back of his study where I could hear the crackle of a fire alight in the grate and feel its unsavory heat burning into my back. "*You* are in this house, because *I* let you be here, I provide you with every luxury a girl of your age could aspire to and in exchange for that I expect—no, I demand—your undivided loyalty and total obedience. This is fair, is it not?"

I nodded, the movement both jarring and unnatural.

"So you wholeheartedly agree?"

Again, I nodded.

"Then tell me, Abigail, do you think you have held up your end of the deal?"

I didn't nod, I shook, fear sending my body trembling from head to foot.

"Well, answer me!" he demanded, his body rounding on me, his glare penetrating my guilt-ridden mind and forcing my eyes downward. My cheeks flamed with the memory of everything Emma and I had done, and the knowledge that he knew it all. That there was no way back now.

Not for me.

Not for Emma.

"At least you have the decency to actually look ashamed of what you have done," he continued, his hands flexing notably at his sides. "You will understand, therefore, that I cannot let this go unpunished, that you need to pay for what you have done?"

Again, I nodded, the tears stinging at my eyes nothing compared to what there would be seconds from now.

"Good, your compliance makes this easier all round," he stated smoothly, his anger ebbing now that he had me where he wanted me. "Take down your underwear."

Even though I knew it was coming, my eyes still flicked pleadingly to his, my immobility giving way to desperation as I prayed on the softening of his mood. "Please, Daddy, I didn't mean for anything to happen—"

"Too late for that, Abi," he said, cutting me off. "Perhaps you should have thought about the repercussions before testing out your new *dykedom* with my fiancée, of all people."

The harsh truth of his words sliced through my racing thoughts, stripping me of any possible reply. Nothing I could say or do was going to make this any better.

"Do it, Abi!" he ordered, his temper flaring with his impatience as he leaned toward me, his hands fisting into the tabletop. "If you don't do it, I will simply do it for you—"

I tensed as he pushed himself away from the desk and made a move for me just as an unidentifiable noise reared up from the direction of the fireplace.

I couldn't make out what it was but it was enough to make him stop and draw away, for that I was grateful.

"For Christ's sake!" he muttered as he stalked off in its direction, leaving me frozen to the spot and unable to turn to look. I heard him rustling with something and then all was quiet again, the only sound the strike of his shoes as he neared me once more.

Before he could even touch me, I worked my panties down to my ankles and righted myself, thankful for the momentary protection of the full-length skirt.

"Glad to see you've seen sense," he said, pausing directly behind me, his voice reverberating through me with its proximity and my heightened state. "Now bend over."

I placed my hands upon the polished wood of the desk and slid them forward, bending my body dutifully at the hip as I went. I didn't rush the move, a ridiculous attempt at prolonging the inevitable I realized.

But then he didn't rush me either, not now that he had me doing as he asked.

"All the way, Abi, you know the drill."

I didn't respond, I knew how he wanted me.

I lowered my upper body until it was planted to the desk, my head resting on its side against the cool surface, my rear forced into a proffered position for his awaiting hand.

"That's a good girl, now raise your skirt."

Clamping my eyes shut, I did as he asked, my hands gathering up the skirt on either side of me until it rested entirely at the base of my back. Not even the heat of the fire was enough to take away the sudden draft across my naked behind, and I could feel my skin prickling in protest.

"Widen them," he commanded, nudging at my feet with his own.

I shuffled them but it wasn't enough. He continued to kick at my feet until the fabric of my white lace panties pulled taut around my ankles.

"Better," he said, backing off.

I tried to banish the image from my mind of him above me, surveying my submissive form, getting me just so. I tried to think of something else, of happier times, anything to transport myself elsewhere to help me get through this but his voice kept dragging me back. "So what say you, Abi, shall I make it twenty-two to cover each of your sinful years in my presence?"

I bit into my lip, and squeezed my eyes tight, I didn't want to give him the satisfaction of hearing a response.

"Answer me," he demanded, his hands shoving away my own so that he could take hold of my dress and shove it higher up my back.

I nodded against the desk, my mouth opening to say "yes" but the sound became a croak as the flat of his hand made stinging contact with my behind. Caught off guard by the timing of his strike, my unprepared body shifted painfully into the desk. The burning friction of the wood against the bare skin of my face instantly stung, whilst my thighs plummeted into the desk edge with bruising force.

"Twenty-two it is," he said gruffly as he moved to strike again.

Blindly, I reached above my head to take hold of the opposite desk edge, seeking its stability to keep my body still and minimize the pain of his next blow.

"You deserve this, don't you?" he declared as strike two hit home, punishingly on target as he made contact with the already stinging flesh.

I fought back the whimper that threatened to erupt, kept my lids clamped shut to hold in the tears that welled.

"*Answer me, God damn you!*"

With sickening acceptance, I nodded, the word "yes" leaving me on a choked sob.

"I can't hear you..." he warned.

"*Yes!*" I yelped in outright pain as he timed his strike with my response, the impact so precise the crack resounded in my ears, the stinging contact ricocheting like shards of heated ice through my welted skin. The tears were too much to contain as they fell across my face to trickle onto the desk beneath me.

"Too right!" he exclaimed, the satisfaction at hearing me break ringing through in his tone.

Another sound came from the fireplace, only this time it persisted. I tried to identify it and then it became horrifyingly obvious, it was someone sobbing!

Fear and mortification rife, I tried to look over my shoulder but he refused to let me, his hand thrusting though my hair, pinning my head to the desk.

"I warned you to be quiet," he bit out, addressing the stranger in the room.

"Please, Edward, *please*, don't do this."

Emma!

I tried to push myself up, to grapple with my skirt and pull it back down but he was too strong. His hands making light work of keeping my body still.

"What did you think would happen?" he threw at her.

"I don't know, I don't know."

I could hear the anguish in her voice, could sense the shaking of her head and the tears that she was spilling.

"Well, now you do. And once this lesson has been taught, neither of you will dare disrespect me again. Isn't that so, Abigail?"

I could feel him looking to me and I nodded my head, the movement restricted beneath the downward pressure of his palm. I prayed that my agreement would be enough, that he would let me go. Let us both go. I couldn't be more humiliated, more pained, than I was right now. As for Emma, she sounded like a sobbing mess. The two of us broken at his hand.

Sure enough, he released my head, my hair falling forward to stick to the damp skin of my face, his downward pressure on my back eased as I sensed him straightening...

The slap that followed was all the more forceful for the sheer surprise of it, the cry it forced from my lungs, throat searingly harsh.

"Edward!" I heard Emma scream just as I heard her move through the room. "Enough!"

"It's enough, when I say it is enough."

"*Use me,*" she pleaded, her voice now directly behind me, right next to *him*. "Do this to me. Not her. It wasn't her fault, it wasn't!"

I felt my stepfather pause mid-strike, and wondered if Emma had physically stopped him.

"You?" he said, as though surprised. "You're offering to take her place?"

"*Yes,*" she said, the hope in her voice clear. "Surely, she has been punished enough now?"

The room fell silent save for our breathing and the shame ringing in my ears.

"Look at her," Emma tried again, "she is terrified of you."

"If she was terrified of me"—his hand fisted into my back—"this would never have happened."

"It's not that simple," she said, "you, of all people, know the power desire can have over us, it makes us do things we shouldn't..."

In my mind's eye, I could see her reaching for my stepfather, her eyes painting a thousand memories for him to think on.

"I know what we did was wrong and I never should have let it happen," she continued. "You have every right to be angry, but you have dealt with her enough, it's time you dealt with me."

The last was said with an air of confidence that took my breath away. She sounded so calm and in control now, like she was working my stepfather and leading him down a path of her choosing.

"Please, Edward," she actually cooed, "maybe we could even have some fun with it..."

The suggestion on the last had the bile rising in my throat. I really didn't want to hear this. But there was no denying it was working. Everything she was saying had his hold over me relaxing again, his fist at my back now the flat of his palm as he rested it against me.

Clearly encouraged, Emma continued, "We could have some real, grown up fun, don't you think?"

Various scenarios involving the two of them flooded my mind, each more sickening than the last. I was trying to push them out when Dad's command reached me. "Abi, you can go."

I had been too busy battling off my disgusting imaginings to register he had already stepped away from me entirely and I now lay hunched over his desk by choice.

Dazed and humiliated, I tried to focus my bleary eyes on him above me but he was looking to where I knew Emma stood and I didn't need to be psychic to know the unsavory thoughts he now entertained. After all, they had just been racing through my own mind. Emma had all but spelled it out for him.

Conflicting emotions raged within me as I scurried backwards off the table. On some level, I was aware of my dress falling to protect my modesty but I was too busy debating what to do to care. Did I just go and abandon Emma or did I stay and protect her? Just like she had done for me.

I risked a look her way and could have laughed at the absurdity of my debate. She didn't even spare me a glance now, her focus entirely on my stepfather as she wrestled control of the situation from him. The mere suggestion that I could be of use at protecting her was ridiculous. She didn't need me. I could see my stepfather practically salivating before her, totally wrapped up in what she was about. If I didn't dislike him so, I could have felt sorry for the way in which she had so readily ensnared him.

"She is just a naive young girl," she purred, her fingers tracing paths along his bare forearms, her face one of seductive warmth, any sign of her earlier distress so non-existent that I almost questioned its actual presence. "Just think what you could do with such strength when handling someone as experienced and as tolerant as me."

My eyes flitted back and forth between them both, my mind trying to carry out a risk assessment on the scene playing out, my conscience still unable to leave her entirely alone but the open seduction just too much to bear.

And then I saw a smile creep into my stepfather's features and before Emma could react, he pounced. Taking up her wrist, he yanked her into his hold, pressing her back against his chest with one arm, while the other slipped across her neck as he spun them both to face me.

Dropping his head into the crook of Emma's shoulder in a typical lover's fashion, his eyes flew to mine, their glint leaving nothing to the imagination. "You know, honey, maybe Abi would like to stay with us..."

Emma's skin turned ashen, her eyes wide as she stared at me. The word "go" silently leaving her lips.

It was enough for me.

She had told me to leave. She had it covered.

My stepfather had made it clear what he would expect if I didn't.

What choice did I have?

Fleeing the room, I didn't dare stop until I was in the sanctity of my bedroom, my head face down in my pillows, my mind trying to force out the rampaging thoughts of what was now happening downstairs. What would he be doing to her? What would she be letting him do?

I shuddered on a sob, tears streaming now that I didn't have to put up a fight.

There was one thing I knew for sure: *Dad can fuck right off!*

The sooner I could get to the bottom of everything, the sooner I could get the hell out of his twisted life and find myself a better one. I didn't need him, or his money, not any more. Whether I had an inheritance or not, it didn't matter, there was no way I could be part of his sadistic world any longer.

Chapter Ten

I DON'T KNOW HOW LONG I lay there for, tossing and turning, not wanting to but waiting all the same for the sound of Emma and Dad to leave the study. It felt like hours but in reality it was probably only one. Their hushed tones as they passed by my door reassuring me that at least they were once more okay together on some level. It didn't stop me feeling sick at the thought of them carrying on as normal after everything that had gone on.

But then what was the alternative? Emma beaten black and blue and kicked to the curb, never to be seen or heard of again?

I didn't want to even think about that.

My thoughts turned to the morning and how things would be. Would Dad treat me like nothing had happened?

I recalled his last words to me and cringed. I didn't want to ever be in that position again. For whatever time I had left in this household, I needed to avoid a repeat at all costs. I needed things to be as normal as possible. And that meant being the good old Abi that ran to his beck-

and-call. Not a foot out of line.

What that meant for the next social engagement with Daniel and his father, I didn't know. Was it too much to hope that I could get out before then?

Probably.

When I finally slept, it was fitful, the entire night a blur of vivid dreams, awake imaginings, and worry over what was to come. None of which helped me wake in a state capable of tackling what I needed to.

The soft light creeping through the curtain indicated the earliness of the hour; Dad, and in all likelihood Emma, would still be asleep.

Keen to take advantage of the temporary solitude, I kicked off the bedsheets and threw on some riding gear. If anything was going to make me feel better and mentally prepared for the day ahead, it would be time in the stables.

Heading across the yard, I could already feel a sense of calm befall me. The crisp morning air carried with it the scent of dewy grass and as I neared, the comforting smell of the stables. The early morning sunshine cast a glow over everything it touched and the birds were out in force. It was easy to forget there was anything wrong when life looked, smelled, and sounded this great.

But as I entered the stable courtyard, I realized that great was downright boring when compared to absolute perfection.

That absolute perfection came in the surprising presence of Emma.

She was stood before Storm's stable door, his muzzle affectionately tickling at her palm as she whispered affectionately to him. Her hair tied loosely at the base of her neck, she wore a white equestrian shirt, beige jodhpurs, and riding boots. I could have swallowed my tongue as I stood there, awestruck by her appeal, my brain lost to the beat of my heart and the fluttering of my belly.

She saw me before I'd had chance to recover and as her eyes met with mine, I saw the flash of appreciation I was starting to become accustomed to where she was concerned.

I wanted to be calm and collected. I wanted to be able to look at her and feel my brain was in control. There was so much I wanted to talk to her about, so much I needed to understand, that I would never get to the bottom of it if I didn't keep a clear head. Yet the chemistry already buzzing between us had other ideas.

"Abi," she breathed, striding toward me. "I am so glad you are here, I wasn't sure when I'd get to see you again, I figured my best chance was to come here in the hope you would too."

She reached out for me and I stepped back, my nerves and mental state wanting to keep her at arm's length.

She spied my move and frowned. "I'm sorry, I didn't mean...I...can we talk?"

I nodded, trying to find my voice and ignore the fact that my body pined for the touch she had offered. The temptation to reach out for her and pull her back was overwhelming, but where that touch would escalate to...it wasn't going to help things, that was for sure, and it certainly wouldn't get the answers I craved.

As if sensing my uneasiness, Storm whinnied, shaking his head and drawing both our attention. It was the excuse I needed to break the growing tension between us and keen to busy my hands with something other than her, I started toward him. She fell into step beside me, her eyes flitting anxiously between Storm and I. She looked like she wanted to say something but dare not.

"You can say whatever it is that's bothering you," I said as I came up alongside Storm, my hand reaching out to gently stroke the side of his neck, loving the solace just the feel of his sleek coat against my palm gave.

I sensed her continued hesitation and worried at just how bad this thing could be. Surely with everything we had endured there could be nothing left to feel this stressed about.

I looked at her then, stood as she was on the other side of Storm's head, her hand mimicking my caress on his other side. She nibbled at her lower lip—a distraction I didn't need!—and caught up a stray strand of her hair to tuck it behind her ear. My gaze dropped instinctively as her shirt separated with the move, the rigidity of the style hadn't given any indication that it remained half unbuttoned but as her arm lifted, the material parted, unveiling the soft, inviting channel between the swell of her breasts, right down to the diamante at the center of her bra. As she lowered her hand, it settled back into position. But it was too late, the damage had been done, my mind was in my panties as the throb kick-started full on.

I tried to stand straighter, to ignore it, to stop thinking on just how appealing she was or just how great I knew it would feel to slip my hand into her shirt right now. Something I was sure she would let me do...

I could feel my resolve pooling at my feet and I shoved my free hand deep into my pocket, focusing my other on caressing Storm.

"Spill it, Emma."

The order came out more brusque than I intended but it had the right effect, spurring her into speaking.

"I wanted to ask if you were okay?"—my eyes shot to hers at the absurdity of the question and she started—"I mean physically? Not mentally...I know you're not mentally."

"Gee, thanks," I said, a smile softening my words. I knew what she was trying to ask.

"I mean, did Edward's, you know, punishment," she cringed over the word, "did it leave you sore?"

My cheeks heated at the reminder of what she had born witness to and I averted my gaze. "Only a little, it would have been a lot worse if you hadn't stopped him when you did."

She cursed under her breath. "I should have stopped it from happening altogether."

"My stepfather is a hard man to stop from doing anything," I said, but then I realized that wasn't strictly true where she was concerned. She could use her womanly form to get exactly what she wanted out of him. The painful memory that came with that thought had the accusatory words flying out of my mouth before I could stop them, "or so I thought."

Our eyes locked above Storm's muzzle, and I wanted to kick myself for being such a bitch. The hurt in her widened gaze stripping me of the higher ground and leaving me feeling ashamed.

"I'm sorry, I just don't get it!" I blurted, the guilt making me angry.

"Get what?"

"How you can be with a bastard like him!"

She looked from me to Storm, her gaze contemplative and I waited for an answer. Seconds ticked by when I thought she would say something, but nothing came. Did she think telling me the truth would put me off? Did she think it too unsavory? After all, the truth couldn't possibly be any worse than the reasons I had been coming up with on my own.

"Look, I just want you to be honest with me," I pressed. "Believe me when I say you can't possibly tell me anything worse than the things I have been thinking."

She blanched.

"Sorry, I didn't mean it to sound like that, I just want to understand what's going on. I want to understand you better. I mean someone as..." I wanted to say special, but revealing that much about how I saw her made me feel vulnerable and uneasy. Instead, I said, "...someone as beautiful and talented as you could surely be with someone that would treat them a lot better."

"Is that how you see me—beautiful and talented?" she smiled then, the warmth coming back into her cheeks, the spark to her eyes well and truly alight.

I blushed. "You're changing the subject."

"Am I?" She was flirting with me now, I could see it in the way she tilted her head to one side and started to toy with the collar of her shirt, taunting me with flashes of her soft, smooth skin once more.

"Please, Emma, just explain it to me," I said, trying to keep my eyes above her neckline, my tongue flicking out to moisten my suddenly dry lips. "I know you can't possibly love him."

"No, I don't pretend to love him," she agreed, her hand moving to distractedly brush up and down the shirt opening.

"And yet you're with him?" I said. *Eyes up! Eyes up!* "Even when he uses you like some sort of plaything? He has you exercised and then demands you to perform for him and his...*associates?*"

I had said too much. In my concentration to remain in control, I'd given away far too much of what I knew. And she picked up on it.

"What do you mean by that?" Her hand at her collar stilled as her eyes scanned my face.

"Look, I know it's none of my business but I..." I faltered, I didn't know what to say. Did I really want to admit that I'd seen her in action the other night? No way! Did I want her to know that I knew my stepfather had criticized her "*performance*"? Hell, no!

Ultimately, the real reason I was drilling into their relationship was because I had feelings for her. Feelings that meant I wanted their relationship over, and her well away from him as soon as possible.

"You what?" she pressed.

Fuck it! "I care about you." The words came tumbling out, a surprising sense of liberation coming with them. To hell with being vulnerable. It felt good to actually be honest with someone. Even if that someone was at the heart of it all. "I can't explain it better than that. What happened yesterday, it's a first for me...there's just something about you..."

I knew I was babbling, but the way she was watching me, her hypnotic green eyes so intent, her mouth pulling me in...I could feel the stress of my confession and the jealous anger stirred by my memories all melting away with her seductive proximity.

"What about Daniel?" she said the words softly, her eyes fixated on my mouth, her gaze flashing with her own obvious arousal.

The realization that she was entertaining the same thoughts as me triggered alarm bells ringing in my mind, even as the throbbing became a persistent ache, a sure sign that I was wet and ready for her. But to give way to it here, in the stable, with workers sure to arrive soon, it would be madness.

Absolute madness.

The idea of madness felt really good...

"So, you going to tell me about Daniel?"

I tore my eyes from her mouth, her words warranting my attention as I realized she didn't want to let the question go. That it was important to her. And in truth, it was important to me too. She needed to understand what had happened with him. It was just one of the things I had been determined to discuss with her at the earliest opportunity. If my brain would just stay on track...

"He was in the right place, at the right time, it didn't...doesn't mean anything," I said, my hand reaching out to catch up the same strand of hair that she had only seconds previous tucked away. I noticed how her head titled into my move, how her lids fluttered closed as I brushed it back and my heart swelled. "I just needed someone to take away the ache you had stirred up in me."

"Are you saying I was the reason you slept with him?" she asked, her voice seductively warm and inviting. Each time her lips moved, I remembered how they felt beneath my own, how her delicate tongue could work me into a frenzy...

"Yes," I said thickly. "I wanted you and couldn't have you. It wasn't about him."

She looked puzzled. "If that's the case, then why seek your stepfather out yesterday to encourage the relationship further?"

"I..." I stopped, what could I say? The truth was I'd been caught off guard while snooping in his study. How would she take that news? I still felt uneasy about having done it myself, but, Christ, if I hadn't I would still be in the dark, completely none the wiser.

"Sorry, it's none of my business either," she hurried out, my hesitation making her visibly uncomfortable. "I just hate to see Edward using you like this."

"That's a bit rich coming from you." I wanted to clamp my hand over my mouth—why did I have to sound so bitter? It wasn't like any of it was her fault.

"Touché," she said, her smile not enough to hide the fleeting look of sadness that befell her face.

I really was turning into a royal bitch.

"Emma, I'm sorry," I said gently. "But you have to see it from my point of view, he is my stepfather, my connection to him wasn't born out of choice, yet you have chosen to be with him, have allowed yourself to be used by him..."

"I know how bad it looks," she sighed, "but I confess when we first got together I didn't realize it would be this bad. Not entirely."

"So now you know what he's like, why stay?"

"You wouldn't understand."

Her eyes pleaded with me to drop it, but I couldn't. "Try me."

She nibbled at her lip once more, her eyes scanning my face as she clearly pondered how I would react.

"Please, Emma, I won't judge you, I just want you to explain it to me, to make me understand."

Her body stiffened and she looked away, her gaze following her hand as she caressed Storm's flank. Eventually she spoke, "When I was little I could want for nothing...my family was very well off, my mother was a multi-millionairess and my father wasn't that dissimilar from your own, except his vice was gambling..."

I listened as she described an idyllic childhood. One where her family surrounded her in love and doted on her every wish. She sounded spoiled rotten—much like me if I was honest—and in spite of her father's gambling habit, her childhood sounded perfect. But then I watched as her expression filled with sadness and the tale turned. Her father started to lose more money than he won, he started to drink and stay away from home.

"...By the time I was fifteen," she continued, "my parents' marriage was on the rocks and they were up to their neck in debt. They left one morning never to return, my father had been drinking heavily the night before and lost control of the car they were in, they went off a cliff..."

"Oh my God, I'm so sorry!" I said, horrified.

She raised her hand in dismissal of my sympathy. "Don't be. My life had been a living hell for years prior to that. They were constantly at each other's throats, dragging me into their squabbles like a pair of children. I'd already run away several times to try and escape. And when they died I was free. I stayed with a distant aunt until my inheritance"—she scoffed over the word—"what was left of it, was handed over and then I tried to survive off it. But it was hard trying to adapt. I wanted desperately to go back to the life of my childhood where money was no issue, that was when I was happiest, but I soon realized that if I wanted to live like that then I needed to find myself a rich partner."

Her eyes lifted to mine as she tried to gauge my reaction. But all I felt right now was sadness, sadness for the little girl lost and the woman she had become.

"And it wasn't hard, I've been lucky in that department," she continued, matter-of-factly. "One man goes and the next comes along. I stay for as long as it works and then I move on. So here I am. I don't pretend to love them, but I do make them happy, in all the ways they care about."

"And you?" I said, thinking on the most important thing to me. "Can you honestly say you are happy?"

Her eyes were so desolate in that moment that I knew the answer for myself.

"Let's just say I've grown up. I was foolish to associate my happiness as a child with the abundance of money. What made me happy was the fact that my family had been happy."

She fixed me with those beautiful green eyes. "Seeing how you live, with all that you have, but without love"—she shook her head in pity—"I can see the sadness in you. Money isn't the answer. Not for either of us."

Her words struck a chord within me. Hadn't I come to the same realization only last night?

"It sure isn't," I said, pain adding an edge to my voice.

"Look, I know you must think me a money-grabbing whore," she said bitterly, and I realized she took my reaction to be one of distaste for her.

"No!" I exclaimed. "I think nothing of the sort! You have no idea how similar we are."

She scoffed. "You're nothing like me. You're young, delightful, miraculously untainted by the scheming world around you."

I laughed. "How can you say that after what I've done, what we've done?"

She gave me a small smile. "You know what I mean."

"I do," I conceded. "But you see I'm no different to you really. I should have run away from my stepfather years ago, but the idea of being without his financial support terrified me. The knowledge that I would have to give all this up and fend for myself—I just couldn't face it. And so I've stayed and allowed myself to be used by him."

Her eyes shot to mine in horror and I realized she'd misunderstood me.

"Not in that way," I said quickly, my tummy turning on the thought. "Last night was the first time he's ever given any indication that he would even go there."

She let go of a shaky breath, her relief both touching and scary, to think how real the possibility had been to her.

"I can't tell you how good it is to hear you say that," she said. "Last night, when I went to bed, I couldn't sleep, I just kept thinking of you both, you know, and what would have happened if you hadn't left when you did..."

She gave a little shiver and broke off.

"I didn't sleep well either," I said, my thoughts turning to what had kept me awake. I couldn't bring myself to ask her what had actually happened after I left. Deep down, I really didn't want or need to know. Once the imaginings became real, I was certain they would be all the more powerful for it.

"I'm sorry."

Her apology surprised me and I realized she had read me perfectly.

"It is what it is," I shrugged, trying to brush it off, wanting to stop the thoughts before they drove questions from me I didn't want to pose.

She eyed me for a while and I started to worry what was coming next, but as her eyes turned back to Storm's flank, she said quietly, "You still haven't told me why you're encouraging the relationship with Daniel."

Her change of subject was a relief but now it left me with the difficult decision as to how much to say.

"It's a long story," I said, and one where I didn't really know where to begin. If I told her I was caught rummaging in Dad's study, she would be bound to ask why and whether I'd discovered anything.

Instinct told me to trust her and I desperately wanted a confidante to share it all with, but I wasn't so naive as to realize that my intense attraction could be clouding my judgment. It wasn't like I had the best track record either, Dr Tate being a prime example of my misplaced trust.

"Please, Abi," she said softly, her face so full of affection and open concern that I had to grit my teeth to stop the swell of emotion bringing tears to my eyes. "You know you can tell me anything, you've learned more about me in the last half hour than anyone I know."

Guilt swamped me. She was right. She had opened up her heart and entrusted me with the story of her past and innermost musings. How could I be doubting her? Even for a second? Mind made up, I admitted, "Dad caught me snooping in his study."

"Snooping?" Her hand at Storm's neck stilled and the horse whinnied, his nose turning to nudge Emma's shoulder. She gave the horse an affectionate pat and then looked back to me, her eyes concerned. "Why would you do something as risky as that?"

"It was an accident really. I came home yesterday and"—my cheeks flamed as I remembered the conversation I had overheard—"well, I could hear you and Dad talking in the study."

She visibly paled, her eyes flicking back to Storm's neck as she too must have recalled the nature of their conversation.

"I didn't mean to eavesdrop," I hurried out apologetically, "but...well, Dad was so loud and I couldn't really believe what I was hearing. That coupled with my bumping into you at Dr Tate's and discovering how he uses him to keep tabs on all his women, well, it had my hackles up and made me realize he was probably a whole lot more devious than I'd given him credit for."

"Fair enough," she said quietly. "But how did you get in his study, that room is always locked."

"I don't know," I admitted. "I came home, heard you talking and before I knew it you were both coming out of the sitting room and I was scared I would get caught listening so I dived in the nearest open doorway which turned out to be the study. I'm guessing he hadn't planned on being out of it for too long."

She nodded. "So you used the opportunity to see if you could learn more about him?"

"Yes."

"And did you?" She looked back at me now, her eyes telling me she had already figured the answer.

"Yes."

"You can trust me, Abi," she said earnestly, her free hand reaching out to caress my upper arm and causing my heart to skip a beat. "I've already decided that I need to work a way out of this relationship so you have nothing to fear from me"—our eyes connected, the sincerity written in her gaze—"*I promise.*"

"I know," I said, my hand dropping from Storm to cover hers upon me. "But first I have to explain about Daniel. You see Dad came back while I was in there and when I tried to sneak away he saw me, assuming I had just come in to find him. Daniel was the first reason I could think of to be seeking him out. Plus I knew his eagerness for us to form a tie would make him less suspicious."

I could see the light of understanding in her eyes and relief consumed me. To know that she believed me made it so much easier. Not that there was a relationship between us that prohibited me from seeing Daniel but I didn't want her thinking I just put myself out there with all and sundry.

I also wanted her to see my feelings toward her were real—genuine and deep. If I was totally honest, I wanted to get through this crap with her by my side and come out the other end together, whole and happy.

No matter how fanciful the notion, I'd never wanted anything more.

"That makes sense," she smiled then. "I must admit I was jealous."

My tummy fluttered. "I did wonder."

"The thought of anyone else touching you"—her eyes dropped to my lips—"tasting you...it drives me crazy."

"I know," I breathed, the sexual current between us positively crackling once more. "I feel the same."

She extracted her hand from beneath mine to cup my jaw, her thumb brushing delicately across my lower lip. Instinctively, my tongue flicked out to make contact with the soft pad and I saw her sharp intake of breath, felt it like it was my own.

"Not here, Emma," I breathed. "The stable hands will be here any minute."

She nodded but her gaze didn't shift. "I get it...but if we're quick...just one kiss."

I went to refuse but the words wouldn't form, instead, I found myself scanning the yard, my eyes and ears concentrating hard on the surroundings for any sign of people.

"In here," I said, taking hold of her hand and lifting the latch on the stable door.

Pushing it open, I gently encouraged Storm to make way for us and led Emma inside. The horses up and down the enclosure snorted at our presence, their bobbing heads visible above the internal partitions. I tried to establish the corner least visible to the outside but Emma wasn't hanging about, she tugged at my hand, pulling me up hard against the stable wall and pinning me to it.

As her mouth hungrily claimed my own, a guttural moan escaped me, the need erupting from within almost painful.

She tore away, her ragged voice whispering: "I'm sorry, I just had to..." and then she was crushing me once more, her tongue flicking languorously against my own, one hand in my hair while her other slipped beneath the fabric of my hoody.

"God, yes," I cried, desperate for her to take control of me, to service the overwhelming need. My knees buckled beneath me and I pressed my shoulders into the wall to steady myself, my body arching into her invasive caress. As her cool fingers climbed higher I remembered my lack of bra—

"Christ!" she gasped as her hand discovered the same, the raw thrill in her voice only serving to drive my need higher. "You are so sexy."

I couldn't even respond. The dampness between my legs almost unbearable as I wanted to lose myself completely to the passion she had evoked.

"Tell me to stop, Abi," she ground out. "If you don't, I won't...I can't..."

I silenced her with my mouth. I didn't care. Anyone could have found us in that moment and I wouldn't have given a shit. Both of her hands were in my top now, her hands groping and squeezing my tits in a desperation that mirrored my own. Without even realizing it, I had maneuvered our legs so that our thighs pressed between the legs of one another, providing a delightful friction as our bodies rode one another, the pleasure building immeasurably.

"Don't stop," I said throatily, one hand moving into her hair while my other grabbed her behind to rock her lower body against my thigh, pushing her climax to come with my own.

"God Abi, I can't...I'm going to..." the words came rasping out of her hungry mouth as I continued to writhe against her. And then she crumpled over me and I followed suit, our orgasms sending powerful spasms racking through our bodies.

Spent and sated, she fell against me and we leaned into the wall, trying to catch our breath.

"I'm sorry," she said eventually, "I never should have, but lately I'm finding it hard to control my instincts where you're concerned."

"Do you hear me complaining?" I asked, my hand combing through her hair as I lifted my other to check the time. People really would be arriving any second now. "But you should go, Emma, I don't want to risk Dad learning that you were here, with me."

"I know," she said, straightening up and righting my clothing as she went. "There, you're as good as new."

She gave me one of her dazzling smiles and I returned it, the afterglow of our brief but crazy encounter still warming me head to toe. "Thank you."

"If anyone sees me, I will tell them I came to request a ride, Edward can't punish me for that," she said, then her eyes flashed as she added, "come to think of it, that's not really a lie either."

"Emma!" I laughed and gave her a playful shove.

"But we still need to find time to talk," she said, serious once more.

I nodded, I really wanted to tell her everything, to have her at least listen while I vented would make me feel so much better.

"Tell you what, Edward has a conference call scheduled for after dinner this evening. We can talk then."

I frowned as I realized dinner would probably be the next time I saw him. We rarely saw one another during the day unless he specifically requested it. "Do you think he will want to see me before then?"

She could see the fear in me and her hand came out to give mine a gentle squeeze. "I wouldn't have thought so, he is so wrapped up in this new business deal that so long as he believes you're doing your all to keep Daniel sweet, he will leave you alone."

"But what about last night? What he said? Has it changed things?" I could feel the panic rising as the questions I'd been dying to ask came rushing to the fore.

She looked away briefly, her expression pained as though remembering something but when her gaze returned she was once again smiling reassuringly. "Just try and behave normally, I think Edward was speaking in the moment, if you fulfill your end of the deal he should leave you well enough alone."

I nodded, her words providing small comfort. "I think I'll stay out of the house today but I'll be back for dinner with you both."

"Okay, just text Edward to let him know so he doesn't think you've gone AWOL."

"I will."

"Good," she paused, her eyes scanning my face, her body hesitant. "So...I should go."

"You should," I agreed, a smile forming as I realized she really didn't want to.

"Right now." Yet her feet remained planted in the hay-covered floor.

"Right now," I nodded, my smile growing.

She shook her head playfully. "Argh! You are such a distraction!"

I laughed at that. "Go then!"

"I'm gone." She gave me a breathtaking smile, her hand reaching out to affectionately nudge my chin. "I'll see you later."

"You will," I agreed, and with that she turned and walked away, leaving me to feast on the captivating sway of her behind in those indecently snug jodhpurs. I really couldn't imagine ever having enough of that body or the wondrous personality contained within.

Storm sidled up next to me, his head nudging for attention once more. Distracted, I placed my palm on the bridge of his nose. "What say you Storm, is it foolish to set my heart on keeping that woman in my life?"

He whinnied, his head bucking playfully.

"I think so too," I said, my gaze following her progress across the courtyard, the realization clear in my head that I would try my damnedest to do just that.

Because life without Emma suddenly didn't feel like any life at all.

Chapter Eleven

I ARRIVED TO DINNER FIRST, my eagerness to get off on the right foot overriding any trepidation at seeing Dad again. Besides, my desperate need to be near Emma was utterly mind-controlling. If I had likened it to a drug craving before, then I was a fully-fledged addict now. My entire being buzzed with awareness as it waited on its next fix, hanging on to her next touch, her next look, her next good word in my ear...

As the door opened, announcing their presence, I stood to greet them. I didn't need to try hard to offer up a welcoming smile, I just had to think of Emma. Only, I couldn't see her, not properly, she was hidden in Dad's shadow, giving me glimpses of her free-flowing hair and a knee-length emerald sun dress.

"Good to see you're on time tonight, Abi," he said, acknowledging my presence with a dip of his head.

"Good evening, Daddy," I responded, working to keep my eyes on him, rather than look past him. "I did promise I would be."

I was referring to the text I had sent him this afternoon following Emma's suggestion. Thankfully, he had acknowledged it with a simple "Glad to hear it", which was enough to tell me that we were at least still on speaking terms.

"So you did," he said, pulling out his seat as Emma finally stepped out from behind him.

I watched as she took up the same chair she had used yesterday, my heart pounding in my ears as I tried to douse the excited stirrings in my gut. But they died of their own accord when she failed to even look at me. Not once.

Did she not feel the same draw as me? Surely even the briefest of looks would have been impossible to resist? Or was she making sure I didn't address her directly, making certain we didn't attract any negative attention from Dad? Whatever the case, she didn't seem right.

I tried to tell myself I was being overly sensitive and reading too much into it, but as I sat back down and her eyes remained purposefully averted, her entire demeanor reticent, I could feel a spark of panic. She really wasn't the same woman she had been that morning. It was more than a desire to evade Dad's wrath or not needing to set eyes on me. She seemed...broken.

Something must have happened between then and now, the question was *what*?

"I didn't say you couldn't speak to one another," Dad ground out, breaking the prolonged silence, his gaze flitting between us as he lifted the wine bottle already open in the middle of the table and poured himself a glass.

"Good evening, Emma," I said, my mind pleading with her to just give me one look, no matter how brief, but there was nothing. And the more I studied her, the more anxious I became, her unusually heavy makeup doing a poor job of putting color in her cheeks. She looked practically ghostly.

"Abi?" Dad said, offering up the bottle.

"Please." I smiled politely as he poured me a glass.

He then looked to Emma and poured her a glass without asking. I wished he had asked, more out of my desire to hear her speak than out of courtesy.

Setting the bottle down, he pinned Emma with a glare. "Cat got your tongue, dear?"

He was being deliberately obtuse and I hated him for it, I had to grit my teeth to stop myself coming to her aid, but then she didn't need it. The look of hatred that she abruptly threw at him, floored even me.

Was she crazy? Did she *want* to anger him further?

"Oh, come now, Emma," he said with bored indifference. "Let's have a nice dinner, you must need it after the afternoon we have just had."

I sensed Emma shudder, her eyes dropping to her plate, and a cold trickle ran down my spine as my suspicions were confirmed. Whatever that afternoon had entailed it must have been truly awful for her to behave so out of character.

I looked back to Dad, but he was already tucking in, relaxed and unfettered by the atmosphere that was close to suffocating me.

"I'm not hungry," Emma said after a pause.

I looked at her, my eyes begging for hers to make contact. "You need to eat," I coaxed.

"Too right, you need to eat!"

Dad's angry interjection made me jump, his words delivering a direct order rather than a thoughtful suggestion. Last night he had requested Emma stop eating for worry over her "weight problem" and now he was ordering her to dig in. The irony wasn't lost on me.

Turns out it wasn't lost on Emma either as she glared at him. "Eat! Don't eat! You want to make up your mind?"

I froze, my whole body posed for an eruption.

But it didn't come.

I chanced a glance at my stepfather.

He leaned back in his chair, wine glass in hand, and met her angry gaze with one of calm contemplation. Then he smiled, the gesture slow and chilling. "You really have more spirit than I ever realized, darling."

Emma was positively vibrating, her eyes throwing daggers, her breathing ragged.

Count to ten...count to ten...I mentally begged her. Hadn't she been the one telling *me* to try and behave normal? Then she goes and loses it!

"Do you know, I think we've actually reached a very agreeable place in our relationship," he continued, his eyes still upon her. "I've had more fun in the last twenty-four hours than I've had in any previous relationship."

"Fun?" Emma asked in disbelief, her voice almost a whisper.

"Why, yes...and it can only get better, don't you think?" His eyes danced as he took momentary delight in the effect his words were having. But then he stilled, his mouth forming a grim line as his eyes hardened and he leaned toward her. "Now eat, before I bloody well make you."

Emma started, alarm widening her eyes as they returned to her plate. Without a word, she reached for her cutlery and with shaky hands, started to fork up her food. I was left to watch in sickening fascination, finding her cowering obedience far more horrifying than her outburst.

"That goes for you too, Abi." He looked to me and I shriveled inside. "I pay good money to have you ladies looked after, so you will eat, God damn you."

I looked down at the hearty pasta dish, Dad's favorite, and what appetite I had, if any, went out the window. My head swam and my tummy turned. I stabbed the pasta with my fork and did as I was told.

I chewed each mouthful with excessive care, keen to avoid it sticking in my fear-constricted throat. I couldn't stop my eyes flitting back to her, my worry magnifying with each stolen glance. What had he done to her?

Conversation ceased completely, emphasizing each chink of glass or cutlery on china. Dad refilled our wine glasses and requested another bottle be brought, remarking that we were both very thirsty that night.

Thirst had nothing to do with it. The wine acted as a lubricant to get the food down and the alcohol eased the top-to-toe tension. I felt like a robot going through the motions of dining. Dad, on the other hand, ate his dinner with gusto and it was no surprise he'd cleared his plate before we'd even got through half.

Wiping his mouth with the napkin, he eventually looked to us both. "Following all that's been said and done recently, I don't think I need to worry over a repeat of yesterday's scandalous affairs, do I?" He gave a sadistic smile at the frozen faces his words summoned. "No, I didn't think so...in that case, I shall leave you ladies alone to finish up, I have a conference call to tend to."

Thank God! I had to work hard to stop the relief shining through.

"The conference call shouldn't last more than an hour," he continued, pushing himself up from the table and looking to Emma as he waited on her for a response.

She didn't give one. Her eyes didn't leave her plate, her manner giving no indication that she had even heard his last few words

He didn't like her ignorance, not one bit. I could see it in his prolonged gaze upon her, as he silently demanded her to look back at him. And when she didn't, he threw his napkin onto his plate and stepped around the table. His fingers reaching to grasp her chin and force her face up at him.

My throat clenched as I heard her swallow a gasp, his fingers inflicting pain as they held her still.

"I'll come and find you afterwards, darling," he said, his hardened stare raining down on her. "I think we should pick up where we left off this afternoon."

I saw the flicker of panic in Emma's face and I couldn't ignore it. Desperate to divert his attention, I blurted, "I was hoping we could talk more of Daniel tonight, Daddy."

He rewarded my suggestion with the briefest of looks and no sign as to whether he believed my idea to be genuine. "I don't think so, Abi.

We can talk tomorrow."

No sooner had he said it, than his focus was back on her and I had to watch as he bent to whisper intimately against her ear.

Taking up my drink, I washed down further words that would only incite trouble and reminded myself he would be gone soon. But whatever he said, it had her body tensing up and her head turning away in distaste. He gave a merciless laugh and yanked her face back to his, crushing her mouth with a horrifyingly invasive kiss.

For fuck's sake!

A cough erupted from within me as the wine caught at the back of my throat and he tore his mouth away to toss me an amused look.

"Aw, Abi, not jealous, are we?"

I tried to give him a look of discomfort, hoping to mask the true emotional turmoil ripping through me. But the effort was wasted; he was no fool, he knew exactly how I felt. I could see it in his sneer-like smile as he turned his attention back to Emma, his hand still fixing her head in place, the brutal pressure of his hold making the surrounding area swell unsightly around his fingers.

"I can't really blame you," he said impassively, his eyes scanning her face in a proprietorial fashion, his palm slipping around the back of her neck.

"I mean, she really is an alluring specimen," he continued, his voice full of stomach-churning appreciation now as he started to toy with her hair, twirling it playfully about his fingers. "She's a feisty one for sure, both in and out of the sack."

I could sense danger on the horizon, could see it in his whimsical manner and the rapid flaring of Emma's nostrils in her otherwise motionless body.

"Such a delightful little vixen, wouldn't you agree, Abi?"

He sent me a fleeting look and I wanted to say something, do something, anything to stop whatever was to come.

But it was all too late.

As his attention returned to Emma, his hand twisted in her hair and he yanked back hard. There was an anguished cry that could have come from me or Emma, I was so distressed I couldn't tell. And he loved it. His sinister smile growing ever bigger.

"But you see, Abi," he said, as he surveyed Emma's unnaturally arched form, her quivering mouth and half closed eyes, "you'd be surprised at just how tame she can be once she accepts who's really in charge...isn't that so, Emma?"

His fist tightened in her hair and she winced, her lips parting on the sound.

He raised his chin a fraction. "I'll take that as a yes."

My eyes stung as I refused to blink, not wanting to leave Emma unguarded for a second. Not that I was any help right now...

Please just go! I wanted to scream.

"So as you can see, Abi, Emma is *my* whore and mine alone." His eyes flicked to me and I could read the challenge I saw there. "She does as I say, when I say. Is that clear?"

I nodded, words failing me completely.

"Good," he said, his pleasure ringing through as he finally released Emma's hair and gave her chin a dismissive flick. "I'll see you shortly, now be good the pair of you."

He laughed on the last, loving how they were wasted words in his view—as if we would dare to be anything else—and turning on his heel, he strode out of the room, the door closing quietly behind him.

I let go of a shaky breath, the word "bastard" coming with it.

My blood was boiling with anger and yet I was immobilized by fear. Had he really gone or was this some cunning ploy so that he could return and catch us in the act? Either way, there was one question burning a hole in my brain that I just couldn't hold in.

"What the *hell* did you ever see in him?"

Chapter Twelve

THE WORDS WERE OUT BEFORE I could rein them in. The full force of my anger toward my stepfather hitting Emma square on.

She looked at me now. Her tormented green depths shaming me with their shock and rising humility over my words. How could I be so heartless? She had already explained herself to me, to make her think on that again when she was so bruised and battered emotionally was downright cruel.

"I'm so sorry, Emma," I hurried out. "I just hate seeing him treat you like this, to speak to you like he does, to have him all over you like that...it makes me sick."

"He only does it in front of you to get a rise out of us," she said quietly. "Especially as he knows deep down it's you I can't get out of my head."

Her startling confession blew me away, a rush of elation making my head spin. She couldn't get *me* out of her head...

"I don't know why you look so surprised," she said. "But then, I guess it makes sense with what you know of me and my relationship with your stepfather and what I do for him...I suppose you think what we've shared is just another fling for me?"

She said it so matter-of-factly, her voice lacking any warmth or emotion that it was almost eerie.

"I'm sorry," I apologized again, wanting desperately to take it all back, to hear her confess her feelings for me without my stepfather overshadowing them. "I want more than anything to believe what we have is special."

"It *was* special," she said, a slight spark to her voice as she corrected my tense. "But your stepfather is a dangerous man, Abi, and I refuse to put you in harm's way anymore."

"What's that supposed to mean?"

"It means I'll do everything I can to help free you of him, but I will not put you at risk by leading you astray any longer."

"Astray? Are you kidding me?" I could feel the panic rising once more, only this time it had nothing to do with my stepfather and everything to do with fear of losing the woman before me. "Emma, you never led me anywhere, I came willingly because my feelings for you are too strong to resist. I have never been so out of control in my life. You fill my head twenty-four seven. You're all I care about—mind, body, and soul. To think you may feel the same, even just a little, makes me so unbelievably happy."

"I know you think your feelings are special but truth is, you just haven't met the right someone yet," she continued, her tone almost distracted. I couldn't believe what I was hearing. Had she not listened to what I had just said? Did she not believe me? She was looking away from me now, her eyes watching her fingers as she toyed mindlessly with her cutlery, her words delivered as though on autopilot... "but you will, Abi, given enough time, you will meet the right person and they will sweep you off your feet. You don't need me—"

"Stop right there, Emma!" I couldn't listen to any more. "Don't assume to tell me how I feel or treat me like a child who doesn't know better. I know how real my feelings are for you and I won't let you push me away."

She lifted her gaze to me, her eyes glittering in the soft light as she considered my words. "I want you to be safe, Abi."

"I know that, but me being safe and our relationship having a future aren't mutually exclusive, you must see that."

Her eyes were plagued with her internal struggle and I saw my chance. "Tell me you don't have feelings for me too, tell me I am not special, tell me you don't want to have a future together and I will drop it now."

"I..." she broke off, her elbows planting into the table as she dropped her face into her hands.

"You what?" I pushed, my confidence growing. "You only have to tell me you don't want me and I will never speak of it again."

"I can't," she said, her eyes lifting beneath her palms, the adoration I saw there taking my breath away. "I can't say any of those things."

"Why?" I asked forcefully, rising out of my seat to walk toward her. "Tell me why, Emma..."

She followed my approach, her eyes almost fearful, her hands lowering to the table as she pressed back into her chair. I knew she was evading my touch, scared that her resolve would crumble on contact and I relished it.

"You know why," she breathed.

I came to rest against the table next to her, aware that she struggled to keep her gaze off my bare legs as I slowly crossed them alongside her, my skirt gathering to mid-thigh with the move.

A small part of me felt cruel to tease her so, but I didn't want her to deny me, to deny us...

"Why don't you tell me?" I said, my hand reaching out to cup her face.

She acted as though stung, her face recoiling from the touch. Confused, I lowered my gaze to where my hand met with her skin and cursed aloud. Beneath my touch was the unmistakable swell and tinge of a fresh bruise running high across her cheekbone. The heavy layer of foundation had been enough to conceal it from afar but now I was up close...

"What did he do to you?" The words were barely audible as they left my lips.

"He showed me who was boss," she replied simply, her eyes closing as she leant into my softened touch.

I shook my head, not wanting to believe it but seeing it all the same.

"Now do you get it? Why I have to push you away?" she whispered, her tone both weary and desperate as she opened her eyes to look back up at me. "I couldn't live with myself if anything more were to happen to you."

My head was still shaking, my mind trying to push out the horrific images of Dad assaulting Emma. Just how had he done it to create such a mark? Had he punched her, slapped her, pushed her down hard upon a surface while...

"Abi, listen to me, please, I am totally crazy about you." She grasped hold of my hand against her face, her voice turning urgent as she realized my head was lost to my thoughts. "*Listen to me,* I have to know you are safe, that I haven't put you at risk, if he did this to you, if he...if he...."

I hushed her. I knew where she was going but, frankly, enough damage had been done. "I think it's a bit late to worry about any of that."

Awash with guilt for events to date, she frowned at me. "Yes, but before I had no idea just how bad he could be. Now I know, I can't possibly put you in that sort of danger." She released her hold over my hand as she added, "No matter how hard these feelings are to suppress."

I could feel the question on the tip of my tongue. "What exactly did he do to you?" but I couldn't form it, as scared as I was to hear the truth. Instead, I looked to the future. "What if I told you the things that I discovered in his study mean that we can both be free of him? That we would have the financial security to have a future together if that is what we wanted?"

She eyed me, her disbelief written in her face, but then she nodded. "I'm listening," she said, her hand coming up to rest against my exposed thigh, the move so casual I wasn't sure she had realized the intimacy of it.

It hadn't gone unnoticed by my body though, the frisson of excitement radiating from her touch had my insides positively thrumming and I lowered my hands to my sides to stabilize myself.

"But I warn you, Abi," she said, the severity of her tone drawing my thoughts out of my panties momentarily to concentrate. "Getting you out of his clutches takes priority over *everything else.*"

That was enough for me. Once she knew the financial security I could offer, I was certain she would come round to my thinking. She had to.

"Fair enough," I said, and relaxing once more to enjoy her touch upon my skin, I plowed straight in. "Like I said to you before, I hadn't meant to go snooping yesterday, I ended up in his study by mistake. But having just come from Dr Tate's where I'd bumped into you, I was totally freaked."

She cringed and my heart went out to her, how she could possibly feel bad for something totally out of her control. "It's not your fault," I said. "It had never occurred to me that Dad would have engaged the doctor's services just to keep tabs on me but seeing, you there, hearing what you had to say, well, it threw so many things into question."

"I shouldn't have said what I did," she remarked, her guilt ringing through in her tone.

"No, I'm glad you did. When I think of the stuff I had been planning on telling Tate in that session"—I gave an involuntary shiver and she circled her fingers against my skin, the caress instantly soothing—"let's just say it's better he didn't hear any of it. And then when I hid in Dad's study, I couldn't ignore the opportunity to learn more. It didn't take me long to scan the files he keeps and find one of interest."

"Which file?" she asked, her curiosity well and truly piqued, her fingers slipping unconsciously—or to my erotically charged self, consciously—higher.

"It was a file on my mother," I said, my voice elevating with my growing arousal as I fought to hurry out the lot for her, hoping it would leave time for more than just words between us. I told her everything: how I'd believed my mother to be penniless, how my inheritance had been kept from me, my suspicions over Dr Tate. And I watched as her expression changed with each part of my tale to one of absolute horror.

"Good God," she exclaimed eventually, her hand stilling against me. "I knew he was devious but I had no idea he would sink as low as to do all this to a child."

I uncrossed my legs, hoping the movement would prompt her to restart her caress. "Well, I'm not exactly a child anymore," I said, my words deliberately suggestive.

"No, you're certainly not," she said, her eyes flashing with blatant interest and causing my heart to leap into my throat, happiness at seeing the old Emma once more adding fuel to the fire already burning inside me. "But that's downright evil."

"I know," I said as I adjusted my leg beneath her palm, coaxing her. "And now I need to get to the bottom of it all, to understand exactly what he has kept from me, how he's done it and what chance I have of getting my inheritance back."

"I see," she said thoughtfully, and to my delight, her fingers started to twirl over my thigh. "But how do we do that without landing you in further trouble?"

"Not just me, you need to stay out of trouble too," I corrected her, subtly gripping at the table edge to stop myself from squirming beneath her like some crazed wanton. "And that's the bit I'm struggling with; the plan needs to be failsafe because God knows what he will do when it all comes to light."

"Yes, we need to be long gone or at least have enough of a hold over him to stop him from hurting us."

"Us..." I repeated. I liked the way it sounded, the way it felt. "Does this mean you will give *us* a chance when all is said and done?"

She considered me, her fingers working their seductive magic against my skin.

"I mean, just think of all the fun we could have together," I pushed, excitement lifting away any remaining anxieties, my eyes flitting briefly to where her hands were working me effortlessly into a frenzy. "Freed from all these constraints, the things we could do together..."

"Like what?" she asked teasingly, her eyes lowering to my bare legs and giving me the encouragement I needed to slide across the table and position myself before her.

"I think I should be asking you that, after all, you're the one with the experience"—brazenly, I parted my legs before her—"I have a feeling you can teach me an awful lot about pleasure..."

"Is that so?" she said, bringing her other hand up to join in, both thighs now reveling in the attention of her delicate touch as she smoothed her palms upward, gently encouraging my thighs to part, my skirt bunching with the move.

"You know it," I said on a moan, getting high on the thrill of being parted before her and knowing what she was capable of next.

She gave a pleasing sigh. "I certainly would enjoy doing this to you on a regular basis, watching you succumb to my touch, shattering around my fingers, my tongue..."

I whimpered. I couldn't help it. Her touch was so soft, so tantalizing, her words and the promise they gave, all serving to work the growing ache. As she reached the top of my thigh, I felt the air sweep across my dampened pussy, my panties parting over the entry of her fingers. I bucked to draw their touch just where I needed them, my legs tensing as the pleasure started to ripple through me.

"So wet for me already baby," she stated, acknowledging the

slickness that enveloped her, her eyes lifting to mine and captivating me with their excited glow.

"Always for you," I gasped as I began to wriggle against her, my hands pressing into the table for support.

"Yes, we would have lots of fun," she said slowly, her thumb circling my throbbing clit while her fingers began to dip inside me, first one finger, then two, then three...it wasn't enough, I needed more...

"More, please, *God, more*," I cried, I was so close, I could feel it building in my toes, my calves, my thighs.

"You want more, baby?"

My head was shaking back and fore, my fast approaching climax leaving me scarce able to draw breath let alone speak.

"Do you know how fucking sexy it is that you're so quick to succumb to me?" she asked hotly.

"Fuck, Emma, I can't...I can't..." I was trying to warn her that I was going to cum, that I couldn't take much more but it was so good, so nice...

"Do you really want more?" she pressed.

I had no idea what more would entail, I was sure she had all her fingers deep inside me now, but to hell with rational thought, more sounded God damn perfect.

"Yes!" I threw my head back with the exclamation, my body arching over the table as I thrust my lower body into her, forcing her further inside.

She cursed, her surprise and pleasure at the extremity of my abandoned state, ringing through on the sound. "Hold your legs apart."

I did as I was told, my body pining for her as she slipped her fingers from within me.

"Good girl," she said, reaching around the table behind me. "Now close your eyes."

I didn't even think to question her, every bit of me desperate for the release I knew was coming.

I sensed her return, her fingers spreading the folds of my pussy apart, and then I felt the cold edge of something hard press against my opening. Before I had chance to understand what she was about, she thrust the object inside me and I cried out with a pleasure so intense that it bordered on painful.

"Go with it, baby," she urged, moving the foreign object within me as my cunt clenched wildly about it, my body reveling in the delicious spasms it provoked.

Keen to identify what it was, I opened my eyes and looked down in lustful awe. Her hand held the bulbous end of a cylindrical candleholder from the table; the remaining inches were buried deep within me. I watched with fascination as she pulled it back, slick with my juices, its intricate pattern sending ripples of pleasure through me and then she plunged it into me once more, her other hand returning to rub at my clit.

"Fuck!" I cried, my head dropping back as I surrendered to the mind-blowing sensation.

My body quickly became accustomed to the size of the object and I couldn't get enough. I thrust against it as I tried to delve it deeper and deeper within me. Loving how it filled me so completely, how the cold metal had my nerve endings alight deep within while her rhythm over my clit became fierce.

My climax was so ferocious that Emma had to hold the candleholder fast inside me as I came, its presence intensifying every spasm of pleasure as I clenched around it.

It was a while before the tremors subsided, but as I came to, Emma slowly withdrew the candleholder and pulled my yielding body into her arms, crushing her lips to mine.

Eventually I tore my mouth from hers, desperate to pose the question: "Does this mean you're going to give *us* a go?"

She laughed. "I would think so."

"Thank God for that," I said, awash with relief as my mind turned to the future and what we had to do next to make it happen. "So we just need to come up with a plan then?"

She studied me intently for a moment and then gave me all the hope I needed: "I think I already have..."

Chapter Thirteen

IT WAS FRIDAY AND EMMA'S plan was well underway.

When she'd first explained her idea, I'd taken some convincing. Not because it wasn't a good plan, it was actually quite brilliant, but more because it scared the bejesus out of me. It was also morally wrong on so many levels.

She proposed that we blackmail James into helping. I had no real qualms about doing that since he was an immoral ass at the best of times. Plus, he was Dad's lawyer and would have access to everything we needed. However, the plan revolved around sex—no huge surprise there since we were talking about James—but still, sex with the sleaze-bag himself was a hard thing to stomach. That being said, it had to be worth it. If all went as planned, he would have no choice but to do everything we asked. It would see us well and truly free of my stepfather at last.

And if it didn't work out...well, I didn't really want to contemplate that...

Dad was currently away on business and James, having received a suggestive invitation from Emma, was coming for drinks. Apparently, he'd been surprised at the invite, but as Emma had predicted, he was more than happy to accept. He had also been keen to keep the rendezvous to himself; both his wife and my stepfather were to be kept in the dark. It couldn't be more perfect.

He was due to arrive in thirty minutes and my tummy was churning with nerves. My role was crucial but my confidence rock bottom.

"You okay?" Emma eyed me over the cold metal clamp she was working at my wrist.

"Not really," I said truthfully. "What if he balks when he sees me?"

She laughed briefly. "You kidding? When he sets eyes on you he's not going to know what's hit him. He will want you so badly that nothing else will matter."

I simply couldn't believe it. "Why would he put his livelihood on the line to have sex with me?"

"For goodness sake, Abi, have you seen yourself in that mirror over there?" She gestured to the opposite wall as she finished up with my wrist.

I looked to the mirror, my reflection gazing back at me and lust slammed into my core. My naked body lay spread-out in a star formation against the stone wall, my wrists and ankles fastened to it via chunky metal clamps. I was imprisoned, I was vulnerable, and yet, I'd never been so turned on. The fear still nagging only magnifying every sensation.

"Nearly done," she breathed, her eyes burning with desire as they locked with mine, their fiery depths projecting a thousand erotic possibilities and sending me weak at the knees, the restraints at my wrists pulling taut as my weight fell into them.

"Christ, I want to fuck you so much right now," she ground out, biting her lip on the last.

"The feeling is mutual," I said, fixated on the salacious sight of her teeth worrying the perfectly plump flesh. I wanted to be the one doing that, the one tasting that...

She gave me a suggestive smile. "You ready for your final accessory?"

I nodded and she lifted a black collar into view. From a D-ring at its center fell two long chains, each sporting a metal clamp at the end. My brain pieced together their purpose and my mouth went dry in anticipation, the telltale wetness now spreading between my legs all the more obvious for the wide-legged stance and lack of underwear.

"Here we go." She pressed against me as she slipped the collar about my neck, the metal chains free-falling down the valley of my breasts, teasing me with their icy contact. Then she pulled on the buckle fastening, tightening it until it was almost unbearable, and I craned my neck to toy with the constriction, marveling at the torturous thrill it gave.

"There's a good girl," she said, standing back and lowering her gaze, her hands reaching out to cup my breasts, the warmth of her touch a heady contrast to the cold metal and bite of the restraints.

She smoothed her palms beneath each curve, taking pleasure at the sight of me under her caress. Then to my dizzying delight, she stroked her thumbs upward and began to roll each aroused nub until I was positively writhing beneath her, sounds I didn't know I could make rippling from my throat.

"You are so perfect," she whispered as she halted the caress.

"Don't stop," I moaned, pleading at her with eyes that could barely focus, all thoughts of the plan going out the window as I craved her continued touch.

"All in good time, baby," she said, and dropping her gaze once more she followed her hand as she raised my left breast, proffering up my eagerly awaiting nipple.

I dropped my gaze too, desperate to feed every bodily sense possible, be it sight, sound, taste, smell, touch...she was capable of inspiring them all. And right now, I was lost to the sight of her taking up one of the dangling clamps, her fingers squeezing the contraption apart like a peg and bringing it to my awaiting nipple. I had a split second to detect the touch of coldness against the highly sensitized skin and then she let go, pain ripping through me as an exhilarating heat exploded in my lower belly. The sensation was so all-consuming that I had barely acknowledged her hand reaching for my other breast, before the second clamp took hold. My body bucked under the powerful onslaught, a cry tearing from me as my breasts thrust forward in false protest.

"That's it, work with it," she commanded, her fingers now trailing down my body.

I was awash with sensation, thrumming head to toe as my nerve endings went into overdrive and I tried to get off on every one.

Glancing up, I caught my reflection in the mirror, saw how wanton I appeared and I knew in that moment that she was right: he was going to want to fuck me senseless.

Emma's eyes locked with mine in the mirror and she gave a devilish grin. "Totally fuckable, what did I tell you?"

She held my heated gaze and lowered her hand to my pussy, slipping her index finger between the folds and testing my readiness. "So wet, baby. So ready."

She started to stroke at me relentlessly and I could do nothing but sway against her, pulling on the restraints, my eyes filled with the erotic display being projected back at me.

The sound of the doorbell shattered the moment and she pulled away. "He's early, that's a good sign."

I moaned. "Please! You can't leave me like this."

"Sorry, baby, but it's time we got this show on the road. Besides, it's good that you're in this heightened state, you will enjoy it all the more...and don't worry, you will be satisfied very soon."

She kissed away my apprehensive expression and then she was gone. Leaving me hanging, desperate to clench my thighs together and come.

Perhaps the wait was all part of the fun for people that took to this kind of sexual pleasure on a regular basis. My body was awash with a multitude of sensations, all culminating in an intense need for release. My tightly-clamped nipples sent sparks of pleasure through me at the slightest movement; the neck restraint was so tight that each time I swallowed it closed around me; my restrained wrists and ankles made my muscles ache and prevented any way of finding release on my own.

Please don't be long, my body begged.

"We have really been looking forward to this..." I could make out Emma's voice approaching. *Thank God!*

"We?" came James' confused response.

"Oh, yes, Abi has been desperate," Emma said lightly as she entered the room.

"Abi!" he exclaimed, following Emma into room.

And then he froze, his eyes registering my naked form against the wall.

"Yes, it's dear sweet Abi, you didn't think I got you here just for my benefit did you...tut-tut."

He didn't respond, his gaze raked over me; shock giving way to blatant appraisal as a desire so raw took over his handsome features that I thought he would come at me there and then.

"It appears that our Abi has a thing for being led astray while daddy is away," Emma said softly. "Don't you, Abi?"

"Yes, mistress," I responded demurely, just as Emma had instructed. She knew exactly what turned James on and we were going to give him that and then some.

"Now the pair of you play nice while I get myself into something more fitting for this evening."

James looked to Emma. "What would you have me do?"

Emma stroked his chin. "I suggest you get over there and get yourself acquainted with that gloriously-exposed pussy. I expect to hear her moaning before I return."

Flicking his behind with her hand in dismissal, she walked off, but not before she pressed record on the video camera secreted next to the door...

Despite my dislike of James, the excitement was quick to build. His rugged good looks and suave demeanor gave him an irresistible quality and if I was honest, my aversion to him had stemmed more from my belief that he would never look twice at me. But he was proving me wrong. There was no doubt that he wanted me right now, and badly if the bulge in his trousers was anything to go by.

I watched him stalk toward me, like a hunter about to take down his prey, his eyes not once leaving my chained body. He undid his tie and tossed it to one side. He unfastened the top buttons of his shirt and let it fall open to display a hint of his tanned torso. He unbuttoned the cuff at one wrist and then the other, folding the sleeves back to his elbow. Every move slow and considered, his muscles rippling beneath the crisp, white fabric of his shirt.

He seemed bigger and stronger than I remembered. Or was it simply that the vulnerability of my current position was warping my view? Whatever the case, the throbbing between my legs had kicked up a notch and I was desperate for him to make his move.

When he finally stopped before me, I couldn't even breathe, the anticipation too much to bear. I watched as he reached out to cup my jaw, his thumb moving to caress my bottom lip. His eyes were now intent on my mouth, their depths gleaming dangerously.

"I've always wondered...always wanted..." His voice trailed off as he dipped his mouth to draw my bottom lip into his, savoring it and then repeating the move. The act so delicate it took me by surprise.

He worked his mouth against me, coaxing me to move with him and I followed his lead, my tongue brushing against his own in a timid gesture. He groaned deep in his throat at the contact, his tongue quick to respond in kind as he crushed his lips to mine. This was more like it! Desire exploded within me and I melted beneath him, losing myself entirely to the aggression of his kiss.

But then he thrust me away, tearing his mouth from my own.

Surprise sent my eyes questioningly to his: What had I done? Why did he stop?

"I need to look at you!" he said desperately, carnal desire darkening his features as he hungrily scanned the length of me.

Raising his hand, he took hold of the chain that hung from my neck and with slow deliberation pulled at the metal, tugging at my nipples and stretching out my breasts. The move sent sparks of painful delight rushing through me and I cried out.

"Fuck me, Abi, did she corrupt you?" he said thickly.

I nodded and he yanked the chain again, his gaze flashing as I cried out once more, my breasts thrusting forward.

"You're so loud," he said, pressing his index finger against my parted lips. "We can't have you alerting the household."

Since the house was deserted save for Emma, it wasn't a problem, but then I figured he was probably acting out some sort of fantasy. I could work with that...

"I can't help it," I said against his finger.

"Then I will have to help you," he said darkly, his hand replacing his finger to gag me as he yanked at the chain once more.

Pain shot through me, rapidly followed by the hedonistic heat of pleasure and I moaned into his hand, tears pricking at the backs of my eyes at the sharp intensity.

"You like that?" he asked, his hand still clamped tightly over my mouth, my breaths coming in rasps as I struggled for air above his palm. "I bet you do, you dirty little whore."

And he did it again; his eyes intent on mine as they glittered with unshed tears beneath him, my cries drowned out by the presence of his hand.

"I'm going to taste every bit of your delicious, virginal body," he said, his voice hoarse as he struggled to control his mounting desire. "And you're not going to be able to do a thing about it."

Releasing the chain, he dropped his mouth to my bound throat to nip and suck at the flesh. I thrashed my head side to side, partly to do his fantasy justice and partly to gain some air through his vice like grip. I felt faint with the heady combination of rising passion and lack of oxygen. It was an intoxicating mix.

"James!" A crack pierced the air and he leapt back with a yelp. "I told you to acquaint yourself with her pussy, not rape her!"

My eyes focused through the haze of desire to see Emma clad head to toe in black PVC and brandishing a whip behind him. It was that which had made contact with James, forcing him back, and now he was on his knees before her.

"I'm sorry, mistress, I lost control," he said, an unexpected hint of fear in his voice.

She walked around him, her heeled black boots clipping the floor, the whip trailing a path around him as she contemplated his bowing form. "Sorry isn't good enough, you shall be punished."

"Yes, mistress."

I watched in awe as this man, whom I had never seen behave anything less than superior and in charge, was now humble and contrite.

"Firstly, you can strip off. It's only fair that I have you both in a similar state of dress."

"Yes, mistress, may I stand?"

"You may."

Emma stopped pacing and stood legs apart observing us. Even though I knew she would be wearing the one piece, it didn't lessen the impact of seeing her in it for the first time. She looked fucking hot! Her hair pulled back in a severe ponytail just as it had been outside Dr Tate's office. Her lips, blood red, were set in a hard line, her eyes glittering severely as she watched us, the whip moving provocatively through her hands. My eyes dropped to the long, black cord and I couldn't help but wonder how it would feel. Would she use it on me?

"Ready, mistress," came James' submissive voice as he came to stand naked between us, his cock standing proud before him.

"I want to see you on your knees before that pussy James."

"Yes, mistress."

He walked toward me and dropped to his knees, his mouth so close that I could feel his breath tickling at the damp hairs of my pussy.

"Good boy. I want you to make her cum with your mouth, James. You have ten minutes. If she doesn't you will be punished."

James took up the task with relish, he used his hands to separate my folds as his mouth covered my clit and then he sucked, the sensation both shocking and arousing beyond measure. He repeated the move, cleaning the area of my juices and then his tongue was on the job, working me like the expert he clearly was.

I didn't think I was going to last five minutes, let alone ten. My eyes flicked to Emma's and I could see she was turned on, enjoying the sight of me losing control. It then became a battle of wits. I wasn't going to come; I wanted to see him punished! Each time my body mounted to the peak, I forced my mind to think on something else.

Finally, Emma announced, "Ten minutes are up, James."

He groaned, his mouth still buried in my pussy, refusing to let up.

"James!" she warned.

Obediently, he stood and stepped back from me, his heated gaze fixed longingly on my lower body.

From behind him, Emma stroked the whip down his back and I watched avidly as she dipped it between his legs to toy with his balls. And then she flicked it back and he braced himself, just as the whip made contact with his backside.

He cried out gruffly and his cock jumped, moisture forming at the tip in his excitement. Emma repeated the move, and each time his erection stood proud, the pre-cum dribbling down his shaft. I licked my lips at the sight and clenched my pussy together in a desperate attempt to satisfy the powerful ache they had stoked up within me.

"Now turn around, James, I want you on your knees doing the same to me. Let's see where you were going wrong."

"Yes, mistress," he said obediently, moving to kneel before her.

Emma positioned one leg on a stool and taking hold of a concealed zip at her crotch, she parted the fabric, spreading herself before him and his eagerly awaiting mouth.

I could see the fire burning in her eyes as she issued him with command after command, controlling every move of his mouth, his tongue, his fingers. All the while, she stroked the whip up and down his form, the gesture both provocative and threatening, a continual reminder that one wrong move and there would be a consequence.

James lapped it up, he was like a cat that had been given the cream and I was jealous. I suddenly wanted that whip on me, her commands to be directed at me. My body throbbed with prolonged need, every bit of it aching from having to fend off my orgasm and witnessing their erotic display before me.

Emma must have sensed the desperation emanating from me as she lifted her heated gaze to mine, the hard tip of the whip handle following her shift in focus and coming to rest at my ankle. I bit my lip, my eyes pleading with her to continue the attention.

Slowly she raised the black leather, teasing a path up my leg, the whip almost but not quite making contact with my crotch before it dropped down the other side. She repeated the move, the touch so soft I had to strain to feel it. I started to writhe and moan, pulling against the restraints as I begged her to bring it against me.

"Poor Abi wants to come, James," she said, taunting me as she moved her hand to his head, pinning him against her crotch as she rode his face, reinforcing to us both that she was in charge, she would determine who got satisfaction and when.

"Please," I begged her, the sound a mere whisper, all my effort focusing on the delicate touch of the whip.

"Let's see how wet she is," she said almost coldly, her domineering demeanor well in place. The whip traveled up my leg and I stilled, the anticipation making me frantic inside.

And, finally, she did it, she slipped the deliciously hard tip between my folds, brushing it against my swollen clit, the sensation so intense my body bucked with it.

"Oh, God! Yes!" I cried, blissful relief coursing through me as she kept the hard leather against me, delving it back and fore and I rode it shamelessly, my climax building rapidly.

And then it was gone, my eyes shot to hers on a whimper and I watched as she brought the handle up to the light to study it.

"Ah, yes, she is very wet," Emma said approvingly. "Come, James, you can lick this clean."

She thrust his head away from her pussy and lowered the handle to his awaiting mouth. His tongue flicked out greedily as he did as she requested. The sight was so fucking erotic that I didn't even pine for the loss of the whip, my eyes drinking in the sight of him tasting me on the black leather like his life depended on it.

"That's enough, James, I think Abi deserves your attention once more."

James turned his hungry gaze to me. "Yes, mistress."

He moved toward me swiftly, dropping straight to his knees to bury himself in my frantically awaiting crotch. Emma followed to stand directly behind him, her attention on my breasts as one by one she tightened the clamps until the sensation became unbearable, my climax at its peak. And then her lips were crushing mine, drowning out my intense cries as I came, my whole body convulsing against the wall under the assault of the pair of them, every bit of me pulsing wildly out of control.

As James sipped every last bit of cum from me, Emma released the nipple clamps and stroked my breasts gently. Leaning into my ear, she whispered, "Fucking beautiful."

I smiled at that.

"Mistress, may I fuck her?"

Emma flinched, flicking her eyes to James and then back to me. I could see her cover slipping as she debated what to say. She had hoped to avoid permitting him that freedom but to me it was a way of sealing his fate. Before he could sense anything amiss, I inclined my head in an attempt to reassure her.

"Very well, undo her restraints first. You can fuck her over that table where I can be afforded a perfect view of you both."

He moved swiftly, his hands undoing my restraints with such haste that I realized it wasn't the first time he had done this. And then he practically dragged me to the table, pushing my body back against it so that I lay with my legs hooked over the edge, one of his hands pressing my shoulder down while the other positioned his cock at the entrance of my pussy.

"Careful, James," came Emma's hard dictatorial voice. "Fucking your friend and employer's stepdaughter could land you in a lot of trouble."

He didn't take his eyes from my face as he said, "What can I say, I'm going to Hell!"

With that, he thrust himself into me hard and groaned as my pussy enveloped him.

"Christ, your cunt is so fucking tight!"

And then he was pounding into me, his hands groping at my breasts, his eyes not once leaving my naked form beneath him.

"I've wanted this for so long!" he growled. "So fucking lo—"

Suddenly the crack of the whip broke through the air and he cried out.

"Don't you come in her, James!"

"I won't...I won't..."

I could see his muscles tensing, his orgasm mounting and then he pulled out, his seed pulsing from his cock across my torso, my breasts, my mouth. He groaned with each spurt, his body racked with the powerful convulsions.

The sight of him crumbling sent my body throbbing and I looked to Emma to see her rubbing at herself...

"Get here," she commanded suddenly and scooting out from under James, I raced to her, dropping to my knees to suck at her throbbing clit, relishing the yelp it caused.

I heard James shift behind me.

"You can get dressed and leave," Emma said, her tone cold and detached as she flicked her whip in his direction.

"Yes, mistress." I was vaguely aware of him moving around and the door opening as he took his exit. We were finally alone.

"Christ, baby, don't stop," she said, her tone softening, her body relaxing as she felt the freedom to let go. Her hands dropped to my hair, clutching me to her. And I groaned against her, the vibration adding to my tongue's caress, sending her to the brink. She screamed out as the waves took her and I moved my hands to her ass so that I could clutch her against my face, determined to prevent the contact from breaking, my mouth working her until she was too sensitive to take the touch.

Dropping to her knees before me she rested her forehead against mine. "Thank you," she whispered.

"It's you that needs thanking. Do you think we got enough?"

She smiled. "We got plenty. There's no way he will deny our request."

Chapter Fourteen

AND HE DIDN'T.

Monday morning at nine, Emma and I were in James' waiting room without an appointment, much to the displeasure of his frosty receptionist—a statuesque blonde that had even the feminist in me questioning the basis on which she had been hired.

"If you could just let him know we are here," Emma insisted, her smile enough to make the saintliest succumb. "I assure you, he will wish to see us."

Without taking her eyes off us, the Ice Queen raised the receiver and spoke discretely to the person at the other end. "I have a Miss Jones and Miss Sawyer wanting to see you, I've explained how busy—"

To her obvious chagrin, she didn't get to finish, the elevated voice at the other end reaching as far as us before cutting off completely.

She looked away as she returned the receiver, her mask of cool professionalism slipping admirably into place. "As you suspected, Miss Jones, Mr. Crane will—"

The door to James' office flew open, halting her mid-flow, and a rather frazzled looking James appeared, his eyes flitting nervously about the waiting room. In fairness to him, we weren't alone, there were four other people waiting to be seen, all of whom now took in the scene before them with apparent interest.

"James, darling!" Emma said sweetly, fluttering toward him, completely unfazed.

He looked to her like a rabbit caught in the headlights and I suddenly felt the urge to laugh, a bubble of nervous hysteria working its way up. It was fascinating to see him so unstuck.

The Ice Queen moved to stand. "I'm sorry, Mr. Crane, but..."

James raised a hand at his receptionist, his face breaking into a smile that only those in the know would deem forced. "Easy, Julia," he said, his other arm reaching out to welcome Emma into a brief embrace, "I always make time for Edward's family."

Julia looked from him to Emma to me, a fleeting look of skepticism marring her perfect features, but then she nodded and relaxed back into her chair, her eyes returning to her computer screen. "Very well, Mr. Crane, I will reshuffle your schedule."

"Good, good," he said, his hand slipping into the small of Emma's back as he encouraged her into his office, his face now turning back to me.

I swallowed, my gaze hitting the stark, gray floor, unable to meet his eyes. This was it. No turning back.

Placing one foot before the other, I forced myself forward. I felt like every pair of eyes in the room followed me, could see right through me to the seedy deeds I had committed only days ago and those that were yet to come. I knew it wasn't possible, that no one could know, but it didn't stop my cheeks flushing shamelessly.

"James," I greeted, my voice unnaturally high, my eyes still floor bound as I passed him by.

"Abigail," he returned, his gravel-like tone reverberating through my ear with his nearness, my shoulder making cursory contact with the solid wall of his chest. The memory of him stripped bare launched to the forefront of my mind and I had to work hard to forget it, to focus on the present and keep my wits about me for the showdown that was about to occur.

Looking to Emma, I found my anchor, her composure and reassuring smile all I needed to continue on. She stood before a large, black desk, her crisp, white blouse and cream designer suit set off beautifully by the light streaming in from the glass walls that ran along two sides of the office. Her hair restrained in a sophisticated bun, her makeup, heavy to conceal her healing injuries, still managed to look natural, only a hint of pink gloss on her perfect mouth.

She was the epitome of professionalism, almost celestial. Such a contrast to our previous rendezvous with James, and no less appealing.

I heard the door click shut behind me as I came to stand alongside Emma and James cleared his throat.

"So, ladies, to what do I owe this pleasure?" he asked as he made his way around the desk, his hand gesturing for us to sit on the white leather chairs vacant for guests.

He looked to us both and adjusted his tie as he sat, the telltale beading of his brow giving away his true feelings on our arrival.

Emma was in no hurry to put him out of his misery. She smoothed her skirt beneath her and lowered herself gracefully into the chair, crossing one leg over the other and interlinking her hands above her knee. I followed suit, knowing full well I couldn't carry off anywhere near as graceful an image, but that didn't mean I couldn't try.

"Well, James, I see no point in us beating around the bush" she said eventually, her confident purr soothing my core. "Abigail has made a startling discovery which we are hoping you can shed further light on."

His eyes flicked to me and I held his gaze, feeding off the increasing apprehension coming off him in waves, a dizzying sense of power befalling me.

"You see she has recently learned that her late mother left her quite a significant inheritance"—his eyes darted back to Emma, his permanent tan blanching with her words—"and that it should have been passed to her last year, when she turned twenty-one."

His eyes flitted between us, his finger working at his collar. "I don't know what you're talking about."

"Come now James, you know all there is to know regarding anything remotely legal involving Edward and the affairs of his family."

Emma looked to me briefly and I gave her a smile, showing her I was more than ready to see this through.

"Look here, Emma...Abigail...I don't know what you think you've dis—"

"I am no fool, James, so I'd appreciate you not treating me like one." Wow! That was me! I'd said that, my voice perfect and even. "I have seen the papers with my own eyes, it's as clear as the guilt written on your face, there is an inheritance that I am entitled to and I want it."

"Guilt?" He gave an uneasy chuckle. "The only thing I feel guilty for is giving into my base instincts where you ladies are concerned. As far as the inheritance goes, I don't like what you are both insinuating."

"We're not insinuating anything, James, just telling you the facts," Emma said calmly. "Abi is entitled to that inheritance and until now it has been kept from her by—"

"By the sanctity of the law," James finished for her, relaxing into his chair, an unnerving sense of calm now befalling him as he studied us both.

I hadn't known what to expect from him when he learned the purpose of our visit, but this really wasn't it.

"The sanctity of the law?" Emma repeated back at him incredulously.

"That's right, Edward has kept control of that trust for a very good reason."

Now it was Emma's turn to laugh, her composure still remarkably intact. "There's no honest reason that can justify keeping it from her and you know it."

I waited with bated breath for his objection, my confidence depleting with every exchange. Could there be a genuine, law-abiding reason for it to have been kept from me? I felt sick.

"Even if that were the case," he said after what felt like an eternity, his voice calm and controlled now as he faced us head on, "what exactly do you hope to achieve by coming here?"

"We want you to give us a copy of all the necessary documentation so that Abigail can stake her claim."

He laughed good and properly at that. "Are you crazy?"

He looked from Emma to me, waiting for one of us to say something, anything...

"Seriously, I'm not going to do that," he said shaking his head. "What do you take me for?"

"I take you for a man who corrupted his best friend's stepdaughter," Emma said abruptly, her cool and business-like demeanor cracking ever so slightly. "And it's one thing for him to pimp me out as and when he feels like it, but from what you know of our dear Edward, do you think he will be so happy where Abigail is concerned?"

She looked at him, her eyes positively ablaze with the suggestion.

"You have no proof," he said trying to sound calm, but the telltale tension in his body told us he was far from it. I told myself to feed on that as I rummaged through my bag for the one thing that was going to get us everything we needed.

"But that's just it," Emma said, reaching a hand out to me. "We've made a copy especially for you..."

With hands that shook, I extracted the disk and passed it to her. She took it, her face one of smiling encouragement and then tossed it onto the desk before him

James stared at it as if someone had just pushed it out of their ass. "I'm far too important to Edward to have such a pitiful thing come between us...I mean, *Christ!* He caught the pair of you up to no good and you're still under his roof, Emma."

I shouldn't have been surprised that Dad had told him about us, but I was, and I didn't like it. Had Dad also told him of how he'd punished us both?

"And what the hell do you think he will do when he learns of your involvement in this?" Edward continued, his anger fueling him now as he tried to crack Emma.

She shrugged. "My relationship with Edward is over anyway, but I won't lose out for long, I'll meet someone else, but you, on the other hand, will lose everything: your best friend, your lucrative business relationship..."

"I don't need Edward to keep me afloat!"

"No, I can imagine that you don't." She scanned the office, the shelves of awards, the accreditations, and the door to the waiting room where his clients awaited their appointments. "But what do you think will happen when this recording goes viral, I mean think about all those people thinking they have an upstanding lawyer representing their best interests...what do you think *they* will do? What do you think the bar will do?"

"Enough!" James shot up from his desk. "*You bitch*, you're one hell of a nasty piece of work!"

"Takes one, to know one," Emma said calmly, rising to her feet. I followed suit, eager to hightail it out of there as soon as possible.

"Was it worth it?" he snapped, pinning me with the ferocity of his gaze. "Defiling yourself in order to blackmail me?"

I fixed my sights on him, determined not to let him see how terrified I truly was. "I don't see what we shared as defiling me as such," I said, my tone casually reflective. "It was more a means to an end...and I think we all enjoyed it, don't you?"

My words shook the bluster out of him as his color heightened at the memories they evoked, his hand shifting distractedly to adjust his crotch.

"Look, James, we're not doing anything wrong," Emma said, her tone softening as she tried to calm the situation. "Abi just wants what she is entitled to. Surely you can understand that?"

James looked to Emma and then to the disk on the desk.

"Please, James," I said, taking Emma's lead and trying to coax him down the right path now that he understood the gravity of the situation he was in. "It's not you we want to hurt. In fact, we don't even want to hurt Dad. I just want what is rightfully mine. No more."

He raised his eyes to me, and combed his fingers through his hair, a gust of air passing noisily through his gritted teeth. "Fine."

"Fine?" I pushed tentatively.

"I will get you what you want."

He held my gaze for moment, his thoughts his own, but then he bent forward and buzzed his receptionist. "Julia, can you come in here a second?"

No sooner than he'd released the button, she swept into the room and I watched with growing relief as he issued her with a list of files to copy.

This was really happening, we were getting the info we needed, the biggest hurdle had been overcome.

As Julia left to carry out his request, he walked around his desk to join us.

"I'd appreciate it if you stayed in here to wait for the copies," he said, his eyes flitting to the waiting room and making his reasoning clear. "She won't be long."

"What is it, James?" Emma said sweetly, stepping toward him. "You wanting a repeat affair? In *your* office of *all* places?"

He quickly backed away, a look of panic on his face. "Hell no, I'm going to get some air," he said, his hand on the door handle already, his other adjusting his persistently defiant crotch. "You two should be gone before I get back."

And then he fled, the door closing loudly behind him.

I turned to Emma, a smile playing about my lips as the buzz of relief coupled with amusement gave me a heady high. "That was cruel."

"But effective," she said giving me a dazzling smile in return, "he truly is ruled by his dick."

"He isn't the only one." The words sprang from my lips as I took in the vision of womanly perfection before me, the spark igniting in my belly as my body swiftly began to demand its next "Emma" dose, and I smiled sheepishly as I added, "If one actually had a dick that is."

"True, I confess, where you are concerned I fare no better."

I looked to her in surprise. "I was talking about me..."

She stepped toward me slowly, her eyes dropping to my mouth, the desire now burning in her gaze holding me prisoner. "And I meant me."

I stopped breathing as I waited on her touch, my skin so sensitized that even the slip of her hand into my hair coaxed a moan from my lips.

"So beautiful..." she said softly, as she brought me toward her, her lips brushing mine with a tenderness that completely belied the fire quickly burning out of control within me.

"We shouldn't, not here," I whispered, even as my mouth parted, her tongue coaxing my own into the sweet cavern of her mouth.

She made a small sound of protest and smiled against my mouth, her forehead coming to rest against mine. "I know, but like I told you, you are impossible to resist."

I gave her a playful push, partly to create some much needed distance before I forgot where we were and forced her to carry on, and partly out of my inability to believe that she could truly mean it, that she found *me* irresistible.

Nothing, not even thoughts of confronting Dad shortly, could wipe the silly grin off my face as we waited on Julia for those much-needed papers. Life was truly looking up.

Chapter Fifteen

A COUPLE OF HOURS LATER, I returned home alone, paperwork in hand. Emma had some stuff to take care of in town and Dad was due to return that afternoon. I planned to go to him with the evidence and hopefully get him to do the right thing without having to involve the law.

Emma wasn't so keen on the idea; she didn't trust him at all, but I had to give him a chance at least. He was still my stepfather. For all his scheming and devious ways, he was the only father figure I had ever known. Involving the law would put him behind bars for sure and I wasn't ready for that.

No, I would simply show him all that James had given me, make him realize that I knew what I was entitled to and what my mother's wishes had been. He wouldn't be able to deny any of it and would have no choice but to hand it over, all of it. Then I could leave him in peace and hope that he would afford me the same.

I should have realized the futility of my plan there and then, not three hours later, when I was stood across from the man himself with nowhere to run...

"Is this all?" my stepfather asked, looking up from the paperwork now strewn across his desk with an almost bored look about his face.

I stared at him in utter disbelief.

I had expected outrage at going behind his back, threats of punishment or similar, even denial, all of which I was prepared to stand off until he was forced to accept that he had no choice but to hand it over.

But his reaction, well, it was no reaction!

He hadn't shown a flicker of emotion as he'd scanned the documents, all stating quite clearly what I was entitled to. He might as well have been scanning the daily news reports or reading up on the weather.

And I couldn't believe the figure in question was too insignificant to warrant his concern, he wasn't so rich that he wouldn't feel the loss of such a sum.

Which meant only one thing...he was about to outplay me...

"So is this what you and my devoted fiancée have been doing all this time?" he said, a disconcerting smile playing about his lips. "Working out a way to finance some sort of scheme to run off together." He chuckled as I shifted uncomfortably in my seat, my fingers twisting in my lap.

Had he had someone watching us the whole time? Did he know of our visit to James? Had someone eavesdropped on our private times together?

He considered me intently as my brain tossed around the possibilities, getting more and more worried by the second.

"You know, I never fixed you for a dyke, Abi."

What! I flinched as though slapped, my head emptying of all coherent thought as my mouth parted instinctively to protest but nothing came out.

"She doesn't love you, you know," he continued, his eyes dancing with his twisted humor. "Whatever she told you, it doesn't mean a thing. She'll chew you up and spit you out. It'll happen even sooner when she realizes that all of this"—he gathered up the papers and tapped them into a neat pile—"it means nothing."

Nothing? How could he say that? How can it possibly mean nothing?

"That's right, Abi," he said, picking up on the fear that must have been written all over my face. "You don't think I kept this from you for my own financial gain do you?"

I shook my head to clear the sudden fog that had descended.

"Oh no, dear, you know me better than that, surely?" His voice positively dripped with affection, his overly compassionate tone sending my blood to ice.

"Why, then?" I asked, my voice a whisper, my head racing to piece it all together.

"Isn't it obvious?" he said, his eyes widening in mock surprise. "I did it to protect you darling...and your estate of course."

"Protect?"

"Of course, Abi," he said, looking away briefly as he opened a drawer to his desk and slipped the stack of papers inside, closing it behind. "I mean, after all, you're simply not fit to inherit."

He looked back at me on the last, positioning his hands on the desk and interlinking them, his brow knitted together in avid concern.

I had to look away, his endearing gaze too sickening to withstand as I repeated his words back. "Not fit?"

"That's right. Dr Tate has been unequivocal in his continued assessment of your mental health."

A tremor ran through me. "I don't understand..." But I did, it all began to make sense now, the pieces falling together with horrifying clarity.

"You mean James didn't tell you when you paid him a visit?" I glanced at him sharply, he did know! "Yes, James kindly called and informed me of your little trip to obtain all of this, but I assure you, it's completely above board."

"*How can it be?*" I erupted, shooting to my feet. "There is nothing wrong with me!"

"Not according to Dr Tate, dear," he returned calmly, his gaze holding mine as he remained seated and relaxed. "In his professional opinion, you're legally incompetent, you poor thing, and it's for that reason I continue to control your assets."

"How could—"

"Now be a good girl and go to your room," he spoke over me, his tone dismissive as he fished out some new documents, "I have some important calls to make."

"You can't do this."

He shot me a warning glare. "You're very much mistaken, Abi, I can do what I like."

"*How could you?*"

"Because I love you, of course."

"Love!" I spat out, rage and outright horror making my body shake from head to toe.

"Yes, darling." He gave me a chilling smile. "And, rest assured, I will take care of Emma, how dare she lead you astray like that."

"You leave Em—"

"Goodbye, Abi."

A large hand closed around my arm and I jumped in surprise, my eyes shooting to see who it was and finding Tom directly behind me. *When in the hell had he come in?*

I tried to prise my arm free, panic well and truly setting in as my thoughts turned to Emma and what he was going to do with her.

"Dr Tate will be arriving shortly, Tom. He will sedate her, but until then, don't let her out of your sight. I'm concerned for her safety."

"Sure thing, boss."

"And take her cell off her, I don't want her thinking she can coax a friend into helping."

I gaped at him in disbelief. This couldn't be happening. He was going to hold me hostage. *No way!*

"You can't do this!" I shrieked, trying to shake Tom off but it was futile, he held me still with one hand while the other frisked me for my phone. Having located it in my back pocket, he pulled it out and tossed the device to my father before dragging me, kicking and screaming, out of the room.

"You can't let him do this to me!" I wailed, writhing in his hold. I tried to turn my head into him, to use my teeth and cause him pain, anything to weaken him enough to get free. But he was a pro. He knew what I was about before I even did and held me fast. He had me in the bedroom in no time and, with a grunt, tossed me onto the bed.

I watched with tear streaked vision as he moved to close the door and pinned himself to it from the inside. His crossed arm stance and faraway stare enough to tell me he wasn't going anywhere. I was trapped.

Incapable of simply lying there and awaiting my fate, I threw myself off the bed and started to pace the room. I had to think of a plan and fast.

My sessions with Dr Tate all made sense now. He was the key. If I could get to him, then I could get a clean bill of health and thus my inheritance.

The question was how...

A confession was hardly likely. I wasn't so naive as to think he would tell me anything.

Could I lean on his moral stance? I almost snorted aloud at the ridiculous notion, the man had already demonstrated he had nothing of the sort.

And then the obvious came to me.

If I had learned anything about my father's associates these last few days, it was that they liked sex. A lot. Especially when there was something untoward about it. All I needed to do was be the "perfect" patient, flick the iPod to record, and wait for him to come to me. It had worked with James after all...

Tom thought nothing of me toying with the music device and true to my father's word, Dr Tate arrived quickly, it just felt like an eternity when under house arrest. When he knocked at the door to announce his presence, Tom sent me a brief look of warning, like I'd attempt to run past him or some other such nonsense, and I scooted to the window to look out at the courtyard below.

I didn't acknowledge Dr Tate as he entered the room, I let the two of them exchange words that I couldn't decipher from my distance and kept my eyes fixed on the world outside.

Eventually the door closed and Dr Tate spoke. "Hello, Abi."

His voice sent the hairs prickling at the back of my neck. I had once found great solace in that deep resonating voice, now it just instilled the bitter taste of betrayal within me.

"Dr Tate," I said, not bothering to turn around.

"I'm sorry to hear of your episode," he said tentatively. "Your father—"

"Stepfather," I corrected at the window, unable to let that go, not anymore.

"Okay," he acquiesced, "your stepfather...he's very concerned about you and insisted I come as soon as possible."

I didn't acknowledge his words, instead I hugged my arms around my body and continued to gaze unseeingly out of the window.

"Come, Abi, please lie down," he coaxed, his hand patting at the bed. "We can talk things through, I have brought you some medication to help calm your troubles. Whatever they are, I'm sure we can make it better together."

I laughed inwardly at that. Had Dad not told him the truth behind my "episode"? Could he really be in the dark? Or was it simply pretense on his part? After all, the doctor had done a perfect job of concealing his involvement with my stepfather's scheming up until now.

Either way, it didn't really matter; I would simply play the ideal patient and be the naïve, confused girl he was accustomed to.

"Please Abi..." he tried again.

This time I turned, the move slow and deliberate as I scanned the room for Tom.

"I've sent him away so that we may have some privacy," Dr Tate said picking up on my intent.

"Thank you," I said, the gratitude in my voice coming easily as I realized we were to be left alone; that no one stood in the way of putting my plan in motion now.

Moving obediently to the bed, I climbed in, my head dropping back against the familiar comfort of the pillows as I allowed myself to relax a little.

"You're welcome." He gave a small chuckle as he looked down at me, his fingers brushing the edge of the bed just millimeters from my own. "The presence of his intimidating stature would hardly make for a very successful therapy session, would it?"

"No," I admitted, my lips turning up a fraction.

He gave me an encouraging smile and what I once believed to be kindness warmed his eyes. It was a harsh reminder of one of the many reasons I'd been so easily sucked in by him.

The pain of betrayal ripped through me anew and I averted my gaze so he couldn't see the hurt in my expression. I needn't have worried as he chose that moment to walk away, his focus on the day chair that I kept in the corner of the room. Testing its weight, he lifted the seat and brought it up alongside the bed.

"I know it's not quite my office, but I'm sure we can make this arrangement just as comfortable," he said, shrugging off his tweed jacket and hooking it over the chair back before heading back to the doorway to collect the briefcase I hadn't even spotted. He brought it to the nightstand and flicked it open, retrieving a bottle of pills and tapping out two.

"You can have one now and the other later," he said looking to me. "I don't want to risk you drifting off when you clearly have a lot to talk about."

There was a gentle tap at the door and I started, my eyes darting from him to the noise and back again.

Please don't be Tom returning.

Spying my panic, he placed a hand upon my own and I had to concentrate hard to leave it there, his touch making me bristle. "It's okay, Abigail, it's just Lily with some water."

Lily! A sudden urge to call out for help, to be in the safety of her presence and be rescued from this situation, was almost my undoing. But the long game stopped me. I also had to remember just how dangerous my stepfather could be, how these people he surrounded himself with could be, it wasn't fair to embroil sweet, lovely, Lily in any of it.

I watched him move to the doorway and open it, his body blocking my view of the other side completely. They exchanged words in tones too hushed to overhear, and then he turned, a tray with a jug and two glasses now in his hold as the door closed discretely behind him.

"There, you see, nothing to worry about," he said reassuringly, his familiar tone, soft and comforting before, now serving to twist the knife in deeper as he headed back to the bedside and placed the tray on the nightstand.

Pouring a glass of water, he picked up one of the pills he'd extracted earlier and offered them both to me. I eyed the small, round pill, a bubble of panic creeping up my throat—was it a sleeping tablet? It looked innocent enough, but then—

"Don't worry, Abi, it's only to help you get settled," he assured me. "I'm not going to hurt you."

What choice did I have?

Cause a scene and make him force it down me or play along and hope it gets me what I need.

Obediently, I raised myself onto my elbow and took them both, knocking back the tablet and chasing it down with the water, accepting that on some level it may actually help with what was to come.

"Thank you," I said quietly, passing the water back to him and lying down again.

"Now, tell me," he said, returning the glass to the nightstand and taking up his seat, one leg crossing over the other. "What has you so troubled?"

I stared at the ceiling a good while, partly to do my role-play justice and partly to work out how I was going to approach this. I decided honesty was the best way to begin, after all, plenty had been going on in my head of late and all of it stemmed from sex.

"I've been having these new...feelings." I hesitated, trying to relay my confusion. "They've been really unsettling."

"Feelings?" he probed. "What kind of feelings?"

"I don't know if I should say."

"Come, Abi, I've known you for over ten years, has there ever been anything you've not been able to tell me?"

"No," I said, trying to ignore the pain that came with that truthful admission.

"Well then, there's your answer."

I nodded and gave him a small smile. "You're right, I know you are."

He leaned back in his chair, his eyes telling me to go on.

"They're of a sexual kind." Heat crept into my cheeks unbidden and I went with it, it would only add to my performance, after all.

"Well, you're of an age now where that's completely natural, Abi."

"This is different," I stressed, "they are so intense and revolve around a woman."

"A woman, you say?"

"And not just any woman, Doctor," I pinned him with my shameful gaze, "it's my father's fiancée."

"I see," he said, propping one arm up by its elbow as he rested his head into his hand, his fingers pressing across his lips in a thoughtful gesture. "Well, have you had such feelings like this before? Toward a woman I mean?"

"No." I swallowed hard as I tried to portray my growing arousal at thoughts of Emma, I recalled her stepping from that car the first time I saw her, her stunning legs bare and outstretched, her body encased in that skimpy white number. "It's just her! Ever since I met her, she's all I think about, my body just burns with this crazy excited need and I can't control it. I know it's wrong, but I just don't care."

"Uh-huh."

He was enthralled with what I was saying, I could hear it in his simple acknowledgement and I was more than happy to continue, feeling a sense of dizzying freedom at being able to voice these truths, to get them off my chest at last. "When she is with me, my mind and body go into overdrive, every bit of me aching to reach for her..."

"You say you want to reach for her?" he remarked with interest. "Could this simply be the girl in you wanting to reach out to a mother figure? Perhaps you are confusing maternal desires with those of a more basic need?"

I almost laughed. "There is nothing motherly about the way I see her, I assure you, Doctor. I truly want to strip her naked and do all sorts of things to her."

He cleared his throat. "Really, Abi—"

"I know, it's simply awful, isn't it? But I just can't help it!" I said, the tempo and ferocity of my words increasing with the thrill of my thoughts. "It's made worse by the fact that I have seen her in action."

"Action?" he queried, his eyebrows raised.

"Yes," I nodded eagerly. "With both men and women! And it drives me crazy!"

"You have?" he said in surprise.

"Yes." I could feel the heat spread in my core as I allowed my mind to wander over the memory of the past few days and what I had really seen of her.

"You've seen her with others?" he probed, a definite edge to his voice now.

"I didn't mean to, it was an accident," I said earnestly, my gaze locking with his and seeing what I hoped to be the heat of arousal reflected there. Not so unaffected now are we, Doctor? Unless the heat stemmed more from embarrassment...

"An accident?"

"Yes, I stumbled upon Daddy and his friends the other night, they were having some kind of orgy"—my eyes widened over the word and I clenched my hands together over my lower belly—"I just couldn't help it, I had to watch...all of it! I saw them having sex, her and this other woman and another man...I just can't get it out of my mind. My body burns with a need so strong, I want to..."

He coughed gently.

"I'm sorry, Dr Tate, I shouldn't even be saying these things," I said, dropping my gaze to my hands to show I was suitably mortified.

"No, no, child, it's fine. It is important that you talk through these feelings."

"But I want to do things to myself constantly, while I think about her and these strangers," I said, parting my hands to trail my fingers across my lower belly, the move subtle but my intent clear and obvious to his watchful eye. "I imagine they are on me, doing things to me, again and again. I know it's wrong but I just can't help it."

In the periphery of my vision, I could see him shift in his seat, his head rolling against the collar of his shirt, indicating his growing discomfort. I just needed to work out whether mounting arousal was to blame or if he was sincerely embarrassed by my tale. I hadn't really considered the possibility that he wouldn't be as sordid as the rest of them...

"Well,"—he cleared his throat again—"this sounds perfectly normal, Abi, seeing her in such a sexual situation would explain why you now have such feelings toward her."

"But that's just part of the problem. I had these feelings before I even suspected this side of her...and now I've seen them...well, I just can't get enough! The real crux of the matter is that no amount of making myself come can help me get past it."

My eyes shot to his, eager to catch his reaction. And I wasn't disappointed. His eyes flashed darkly, his hand dropping to his upper thigh—a discrete attempt to conceal his crotch, I hoped!

"How many times a week would you say you're enjoying yourself in this way?" he asked, his eyes flicking frequently to my fingers as I continued to caress my lower belly.

"A week?" I laughed softly. "It's at least twice a day, Doctor. Like I said, it's not normal, it's consuming me."

"I see," he said thickly.

"What am I to do?" I whispered in desperation.

"Have you considered working through this with a partner?"

"Like who, Dr Tate? I don't want a relationship with another woman. I can't very well go to her and I'm not sure a man would be able to do anything with me when she is all I think about."

He studied me intently, his eyes beginning to burn with mounting passion as he took in my restless state and wandering fingers.

"I'd like to try something, Abi," he said eventually. "Do you trust me?"

I nodded, looking up at him in wide-eyed innocence. "Completely, Dr Tate, you know me better than anyone."

He swallowed hard. "That's good to hear, now close your eyes."

I did as he asked and heard him move away. Where was he going?

The faint click of my door being locked answered that question and I listened intently as he moved about the room, every sense heightened as I strained to hear.

"Now take a deep steadying breath, Abi," his voice was right next to me once more. "That's it, just like I have taught you."

I inhaled deeply, aware of my breasts inflating with the move, and I imagined his eyes hungrily drinking me in, freed of the constraints of having me watch him.

"There's a good girl, now when you're ready why don't you tell me what you see when you think of her?" he said softly. "One of your fantasies perhaps?"

I nodded, taking another breath as I began painting the picture in my mind's eye and recounting it to him. "I imagine passing by her bedroom door…it's ajar and I can see her…she is standing before a mirror, undressing…her reflection giving me the perfect view of her front…" I shimmy back against the plush fabric of the bed, showing him how at ease I feel and how wrapped up I am in my imaginings as I continue. "I know I should keep on walking but my body refuses to budge, my eyes unable to take their gaze off her…I watch as she unbuttons her top, it's a white chiffon blouse that hints at the delicate lace bra beneath. Her fingers work so slowly over the buttons, it's as though she knows I am watching but I haven't made a sound and she hasn't given any sign that she has spotted me. She pulls the fabric out of her skirt and then brushes it from her shoulders, letting it slip down her arms and float to the floor. As she raises her hands to the clasp at her back, her eyes collide with mine in the mirror and I freeze, unable to speak, scared of what she will do. But then she smiles, her eyes warm and inviting, her hands still at her back and, to my surprise and pleasure, she continues to unfasten it, dropping the fabric to the floor, her bare breasts now freed to my appreciative gaze. My eyes don't know where to look, to hold her seductive gaze or have their fill of her beautiful body. They are just so full, so pert they make my mouth dry with longing…"

I felt rather than heard him move, his fingers closing around the buttons on my blouse.

"What are you doing, Doctor?" I whispered, my eyes still shut.

"Shhh," he soothed, his hands starting to undo the buttons. "Just concentrate on your fantasy, Abi, I'm going to help you with it."

"But…"

"It can be our secret, Abi," he insisted, his hands gently tugging my blouse out of my jeans to get at the last few buttons. "I promise I will make it all better."

"You will?"

"I will," he promised. "Now continue…"

I swallowed back my mounting nerves and to my surprise, arousal. I hadn't anticipated actually enjoying this.

"Her reflection beckons me and I go willingly, her hand taking hold of my own to pull me before her. She positions herself behind me so that we both face the mirror and slowly she begins to remove my clothing...all the while our eyes are fixed on our reflection, of her hands as they take hold of the hem of my top and lift it over my head..."

I felt the bed dip with the arrival of his weight, his hands parting my shirt. The air caught in my lungs as my body basked in the sudden exposure to the air, the thrill sending my nipples hard against the lace of my bra.

"And?" he prompted softly.

I let go of a shaky breath, trying to concentrate through the exhilarating mass of excited nerve endings that were waiting on his next move.

"She strokes her fingers down my throat, across my shoulders...she slips them beneath my bra straps and teases them down my arms..."

His hands followed my tale, one hand lifting my shoulders, the other pulling my blouse and bra straps down to my elbows before lowering me back to the bed.

The sheer wickedness of what he was doing, of what I was letting him do, had my body pulsing wildly, it was all I could do to continue on. "...she brings her hands inwards and slips them beneath my bra..."

I moaned as he did just that, his hands cupping my breasts, his rough skin grazing my nipple...

"...my breasts are on fire at her touch as she massages and kneads them before lifting them out, exposing them to our watchful eyes...and then she toys with each nipple...she rolls them in her thumb and forefinger..."

Dr Tate's actions followed me word for word and the dampness spread between my legs, my breathing coming in heavy pants as I gave myself up to his caress.

"What does she do next, Abi?" he asked, his voice hoarse as he struggled to maintain his control.

"She lowers her hands over my torso."

He moved one hand down across my belly, the warmth of his palm setting my skin on fire. "Like this?"

"Yes," I breathed.

"And then does she unbutton your jeans?" he asked gruffly, his impatience to get to my cunt evident as he made swift work of the fastening without waiting for a response.

I nodded anyway, I felt I should, the sexual excitement blurring with sudden tiredness and making everything surreal.

"That pill should be working its magic, Abi, how do you feel?"

"Nice...sleepy..." I replied, my tone distant as I sighed contentedly at the warmth enveloping my body.

"Good," he said slackening off my jeans just enough to permit his hand to slip into my panties.

He groaned with pleasure as he fingered me. "There's a good girl, you're all nice and wet."

He stroked at my clit, the motion gentle and hypnotic. I felt like I was floating on a cloud somewhere and in the distance there was this deliciously growing tension.

He shifted off the bed, the move accompanied by the sound of a zipper being undone and then he was back, his hands taking hold of the waistband of my panties and jeans to pull them down to my calves.

"There's a good girl, you rest," he said as he moved his hands to my bare knees and encouraged them apart, opening my pliant body up to him.

"Beautiful," he said under his breath and then his hand was immediately upon me, toying with my pussy, his fingers slipping deep inside repeatedly while his thumb massaged my clit.

Back and fore, he worked me, his move so precise and erotic. I moaned faintly as the pleasure built within, the noise joined by the unmistakable pumping sound of his hand over his cock.

"There's a good girl." His voice was strained as his hands continued to drive us both in unison. "I told you I'd make it all better."

I was vaguely aware of my body giving up to the tension, spiraling and shattering under his relentless rhythm.

"Such a good...fucking...*girl!*" The words came in time with his thrusts, the last leaving him on a groan as his cum spurted all over my naked thighs and torso.

Silence descended, save for his ragged breathing, and I listened as he fought to bring it back under control, trying to stay alert as to what he was about. But it was no good; I could feel my attention slipping, sleep taking over as my sated body relaxed into the comfort of the bed...

"There, that should help." His words roused me but I had no idea whether I'd been asleep or not, I felt incapable of opening my eyes, let alone speaking.

"Now for that final pill. Say ah." He lifted my head and parted my lips, popping the pill into my mouth followed by a trickle of water.

Dutifully, I swallowed it all down, grateful to feel the pillow beneath my head once more...

Chapter Sixteen

I AWOKE WITH A START, my head a disorientated mess. Emma had haunted my dreams, her screams reverberating through my mind with no let-up. I'd been unable to do anything but listen, my body heavy and unwilling to do my bidding, my brain incapable of coherent thought.

But now I was awake, I worried that the noise hadn't come from my dreams at all. The memory of them too real to have been created by my mind.

I swung my feet off the bed and sat up, my mind playing catch up as I tried to shake off the haze.

And then I remembered.

Everything.

It all came flooding back: James, my stepfather, Emma, Dr Tate...I checked my clothes; they were completely fastened, nothing amiss. The doctor had been very careful to clean me up and leave me like nothing had ever happened. But then...had it *actually* happened? Or was it all just a crazy dream too?

With sickening confusion, I leaned over the bed and reached for the iPod, half expecting to find nothing. But sure enough there it was, the new recording ready for review. I pressed play and listened, skipping ahead to make sure I had captured it all.

It hadn't missed a beat, every sordid moment captured with enough clarity to serve the purpose I had in mind. Before I ran the risk of losing it, I emailed the file for backup and gingerly got to my feet. I didn't have time to wait for the remnants of the drugs to wear off, I had to get moving, I had to find Emma.

Heading to the door, I listened for anyone on the other side. It was quiet. My stepfather was probably content that I was drugged out of my mind. And if I was honest, I really still was.

Opening the door, the empty hallway was a welcome sight and I headed to Dad's quarters in search of her. Every sense was heightened in fear of what I might find. I simply couldn't shake the sound of those screams. I could only hope that their lucidity was the result of the drugs and my overactive imagination, that they had never actually taken place in this house, while I was incapacitated. My head swam with all sorts of ghastly scenarios involving my stepfather administering a variety of punishments, of Emma's body bruised and battered at his hand, that I almost fell across the threshold to his room, my legs giving out beneath me. I caught hold of the doorframe to steady myself and kicked open the door fully.

The place was deserted; there was no sign of either of them.

Pushing off the doorframe, I drifted across the room, my sights set on the entrance to the dressing room reserved for my stepfather's woman. I don't know why I needed to see it, but the desire to be surrounded by things that belonged to her pulled me in. I held my breath as I swung open the doors.

The pain was instant, the force so strong it sent me to my knees.

The room was completely bare. All trace of her gone, as though she'd never existed, the sense of loss spearing me through the heart and turning my gut to lead. How was I going to find her? How was I to know if she was okay? Had my stepfather cleared out her stuff or had Emma got there first and made a break for it?

I hugged my arms around me, trying in vain to ease the pain. Now wasn't the time for debate, whatever had happened I needed to get out of the house. Getting to my feet, I turned to leave, but the sign of a blemish on the otherwise immaculate cream carpet caught my eye. Alarm bells rang as I immediately hit the light. The mark was red, a deep shade. I dropped back to my knees for a closer look, ice racing through my veins as I realized my worst fear: it was blood.

He wouldn't kill her, I quickly told myself, he wasn't a murderer.

But how could I know for sure? I hadn't taken him for a man to steal my inheritance either. And those screams, they'd been so real...

Shooting to my feet I raced through the house as fast as my drug-inflicted body would allow me. I knew I shouldn't drive but I didn't feel I had a choice. I had to track Emma down and fast. The only way I could think to do that was through Dr Tate, he must have a correspondence address for her, Emma didn't live with Dad all the time. Grabbing my car keys and pocketing my iPod, I flew out the door.

I drove to his office building on auto-pilot, every effort going into making sure I drove safely and pushing out all thoughts of "What if?". It was six in the morning when I arrived in the parking lot. He wouldn't be in yet, his first appointment slot was seven-thirty. I intended on getting to him first. I would use the recording to make him hand over Emma's personal details and certify me as sane, or whatever it was that I needed to prove that I could inherit. Then I would go straight to Emma's and seek her out.

Settling back into the driver's seat, I could feel my eyes closing, the hangover from the drugs weighing me down. Pulling out my iPod, I set the alarm, afraid that I would run the risk of falling asleep and missing his arrival. Satisfied it would wake me within the hour, I used my jacket as a blanket and let sleep take over.

My phone woke me in plenty of time to catch his car turning into the parking lot at seven-fifteen. I had to stop myself from jumping out too early. I wanted him away from his car before I sprang upon him. I didn't want to risk him trying to bolt.

He had blipped his car and was halfway across the lot when I stepped into his path.

"Abi?" he said in surprise, a hint of fear in his tone.

"Dr Tate."

"Should you be driving?" his eyes scanned the lot as though looking for someone to have accompanied me. "I wouldn't expect you to be—"

"I don't have time for your concerns, Dr Tate," I said sharply. "I'm in a hurry, can we take this inside?"

He hesitated but as another car pulled into the lot, his nerves got the better of him and he gestured for me to precede him into the building. We didn't speak as we walked through the various corridors that led to his office. There weren't many people about and I wanted to be in the sanctity of his office in close proximity of his arriving clients and his receptionist before I pushed him to provide all that I wanted.

As we entered his waiting area, his receptionist was already in situ, a coffee for her boss ready and waiting. She greeted us both politely, any curiosity at my presence well masked.

"Thank you, Cara," he said, taking up his drink with a smile that didn't quite reach his eye. "Would you care for a drink, Abigail?"

"Not particularly," I said, the coldness to my tone earning a questioning glance from the receptionist.

"Very well," he said. "Can you delay my seven-thirty appointment please, Cara? Abigail and I are not to be disturbed."

"Of course," she replied, her focus turning to the computer screen as she began to tap away. I could feel her gaze flicking back to me as I followed Dr Tate into his office. I knew her brain would be doing overtime trying to guess my reason for being there but I didn't care. Having her present made me feel safe.

"Take a seat, Abigail," he said to me as he closed the door behind me.

"I'd rather stand, if you don't mind." Not that I truly cared if it did bother him, the words just came out automatically.

"As you wish," he said, turning away and heading to his desk. "If you don't mind, I'm going to take a seat though."

"Suit yourself, you're probably going to need it." He paused halfway to taking his seat, his eyes flicking nervously to me before he continued back, unbuttoning his jacket as he sat. I could see him fighting for composure but the pulse working in his clamped jaw spoke volumes.

"So, are you going to tell me what brings you here?" he said, casually leaning back in his chair.

Here we go. I kept my steady gaze on him and, without ceremony, issued my first command. "I want you to get me Emma's personal details."

His eyes widened with surprise and he shook his head. "I can't do that."

"I've not finished, Dr Tate. I also want you to certify me as mentally sound so that I can inherit what is rightfully mine."

His eyebrows positively hit the roof; if he'd been surprised before, then he was stunned speechless now.

"Look, Doctor, I have somewhere else to be so if you can—"

"Now, Abi," he cut over me, giving a nervous chuckle, "I'm not sure what you think is going on here, but I assure—"

"Save it, Doctor! If you don't get me those things immediately I will make public this rather interesting recording I have of our session last night."

He turned white as a sheet, his body flinging forward in his seat as his hands planted into the desk before him. "A recording?"

"Yes," I said, taking great satisfaction in the effect my words were having and the amazing control to my voice as I successfully hid the rampaging butterflies in my belly.

His brow furrowed. "An actual recording?"

Now he just looked stupid and I had to resist the temptation to tell him as much. "Yes, you must be familiar with them since you often record sessions with your patients, do you not?"

He dropped his gaze, his eyes flitting about his desk as a look of sheer panic befell him. My confidence sky high, I pressed further. "But, you see, in this recording you quite clearly abuse your position. Several times over in fact. It will definitely see you struck off, completely ruined, for sure, and there will undoubtedly be some form of legal suit. So, you see, the choice is yours, give me what I want or this will be circulated to all and sundry."

He pushed himself back in his chair, forcing himself to appear untroubled I surmised, and his eyes returned to mine. I knew he was about to call my bluff even before he spoke, he had to try and I expected no less. "Do you take me as some kind of fool, Abi? Why would I believe that you have such a recording?"

I took the iPod out of my pocket along with a portable speaker and watched his face turn from forced calm to dawning horror to outright panic as the recording played out. It started right in the middle where the distinctive sound of his wanking interlaced with the words coming out of his mouth. It was perfect.

"And this isn't my only copy," I assured him. "Don't be fool enough to think I'd risk bringing the only one I had."

He studied me, long and hard, the tension in the air palpable as the gravity of the situation really started to hit home for him. The only sound in the room was the clock ticking away, an incessant reminder that I didn't have time to hang about but I didn't dare press him further. Ultimately, we both knew he had no choice.

The shrill sound of the phone ringing suddenly pierced the air and we both started.

"Christ, I told her we weren't to be disturbed!" he exclaimed, ramming the intercom button. "What is it?"

"Apologies, Dr Tate, but I have Mr. Sawyer on the line"—the

doctor's eyes shot to mine—"he says it's urgent."

Shit! Why was my stepfather ringing? Had he already discovered I was AWOL? I nodded at the doctor to take the call. "Don't you say a word out of line."

The stress in his gaze was enough to assure me that I had him by the balls; he wasn't going to say anything, not just yet anyway.

"Very well, put him through, Cara."

He snatched up the receiver and thrust his free hand through his hair, his frenzied gaze fixed on the iPod in my hand.

"Edward," he said in brusque greeting, and then he turned away, clearly unable to face the evidence of his perverted act while speaking to my stepfather. He was quiet for a while, listening to whatever Dad was telling him and then he finally spoke. "No, she should be out for at least another two hours with the dose she had"—he flicked his eyes at me briefly—"where are you? No, I wouldn't worry, I'm sure she will be out of it when you return. Not a problem. Goodbye."

Slowly he hung up the receiver, his mind elsewhere, probably pondering a way out of the mess he had found himself in.

"Where is he?" I asked, forcing his attention back to the present.

"He didn't say, just that he had some business to take care of and that he was on his way home, he'd had to leave you unattended and was concerned that you'd make a break for it."

I smiled scornfully. "Concerned, was he? How very noble."

"He is your stepfather, Abi."

"I'm not here for a session, Dr Tate, I want those documents and I want them now." I raised the iPod in my hand, an attempt to spur him into action.

"Okay, okay," he said, raising his hands to me in an "I'm on it" gesture. His attention turned to the computer screen and busily he typed away, his eyes permanently fixed to the monitor as he purposefully avoided my gaze. Not that I cared. I just wanted to get out of there as soon as possible.

Before I knew it, the printer fired up and several pages spurted out.

He snatched them up, scribbled on one and tossed them across the desk at me.

"Your mental health..." he said, by way of explanation before pressing the intercom for his receptionist. "Cara, can you get me the file on Miss Emma Jones?"

"Yes, Dr Tate."

"Quickly, please."

Mere minutes passed and his receptionist swept into the room, file in hand. She eyed me suspiciously, taking in my standing form and the Doctor's harried state. She was astute enough to know that something was amiss but too professional to question either of us as she took her leave.

Pulling out the top sheet containing Emma's personal details, he tossed it at me. "Write down what you require and leave."

Part of me wanted to insist on the whole file, curiosity about the woman I was crazy about making me thirsty to know everything, but I didn't push my luck. I jotted down her address and number, picked up the official document he had drawn up and walked to the door.

"For what it's worth, Abi, your stepfather does care about you in his own way."

I laughed derisively.

"Just as you cared for me, Dr Tate," I flung over my shoulder, pulling open the door and walking out.

I continued to walk right up until I reached the parking lot and then I ran. Desperation to get to Emma's home to see if she was there, to see if she was okay, taking over.

Swinging into the seat of my car, I checked the location of her apartment block. It was in the city, not far from here. Ramming the car into reverse, I sped out of the parking space and exited the lot, my focus solely on getting to her as soon as possible.

Chapter Seventeen

HALF AN HOUR LATER I was scaling Emma's fire escape and climbing through her open window. I had tried buzzing her apartment but there had been no response and I was out of my mind with worry. If someone called the cops at the sight of me breaking in, then so be it. I had a good enough story to tell, that was for sure. Any sense of loyalty to the man that had been my father figure was well and truly gone, he could be locked up for life now and I wouldn't care.

As soon as my feet hit the ground, I straightened and scanned my surroundings. I was in the living area. The kitchen/diner was to my left, the main apartment door straight ahead and two further doors were to my right. One, I assumed, would be to her bedroom and one to the bathroom. There were no sounds in the flat, other than those that came from outside and the adjoining tenants.

"Emma?" I called out tentatively, trying to calm my racing pulse. "Emma, are you here? It's me, Abi."

"Abi?" Her voice was so quiet I almost missed it.

"Emma?" I raced to one of the doors, swinging it open. It was the bedroom. The bed was a ruffled mess but empty, there were clothes strewn on the floor along with an open suitcase, but no Emma.

"Emma, where are you?"

"In here." The sound came from the other door and in my desperation I flung it open, not thinking to knock. There she was, her body cocooned in a deep bubble bath. Relief swept through me but then I saw her properly: a bust lip, a bruised jaw and a graze across her right knuckle. And those were just the bits I could see.

"Baby!" I raced to the tub and knelt beside it, my hand moving to cover hers. Pain like I had never known ripped through me. *The bastard had done this to her!*

"Hey, darling, it's okay, please don't cry," she said gently, her hand coming up to stroke the crazy mass of hair from my face.

I wiped at my eyes to rid them of the tears I'd unknowingly shed, but it was no use, they fell relentlessly as the true horror of what my stepfather had done was before me. "How could he do this to you? How could he be so evil? I'm so, so sorry."

"Hey, you don't have anything to be sorry for," she soothed. "I only have myself to blame."

"How can you say that?" I said, my voice full of anguish and guilt.

She gave a small, knowing smile. "You know how, it's just like you said, I never should have got involved with him in the first place."

"Oh, Emma," I shook my head, my tears falling hard and fast as I bowed my head to rest against her own.

"Please don't cry," she said again, wincing as she tried to sit up in the bath, the reaction enough to tell me that her body was indeed sporting similar injuries to her face.

Concern taking over my grief, I raised my head to look at her. "You need medical attention."

"I'll be okay," she said trying to smile and failing pathetically. "It's nothing an ice pack or two won't heal. What about you, though? Edward told me it was all a wasted effort, that he'd had you certified as insane or some such nonsense..."

I could hear the rising panic in her voice and see her body stiffening with the stress of her thoughts, her face contorting with pain as the tension aggravated her wounds.

"Shh, baby, don't worry about that right now." I said, my hand gently squeezing her own. Now was not the time. She didn't have the strength to go through it all and, more importantly, I needed to get us out of the flat before my stepfather tracked us down. God knew how far he would go if he found us together. There would be plenty of time to explain everything when we were safely away.

"How can I not worry?" she stared up at me, her captivating green orbs wide with concern. "From the moment I met you, I've wanted to look after you."

Her words warmed me to the core and instinctively I reached for her, my fingers nudging her lips to mine as I pressed a gentle kiss to the corner of her mouth, the side untouched by my stepfather and his thugs.

"We can talk about it all later, let's get you out of the bath first," I said, my voice soft and encouraging. "Everything will be all right"—she eyed me doubtfully—"I promise."

She still didn't look convinced but at least she didn't object, her hand coming out for my own as she started to stand. Helping her out, I had to bite back a gasp as the bubbles slid down her body and unveiled patch after patch of fresh bruising.

Christ, they must have used her like a punch bag!

The imagery brought bile rising in my throat and I swallowed it down. Turning away to take up the largest towel I could find, I wrapped it around her, careful not to touch her too hard, and led her into the bedroom.

She was shivering uncontrollably beneath my palms as I set her down on the edge of the bed and I hurried to draw the quilt up and over her shoulders.

"Thank you," she said, her voice trembling, her legs jittering up and down as she worked to warm herself up.

"I just want to check you over," I said to her gently, my hands rubbing carefully up and down her arms.

She gave a violent shudder that had me biting back further tears and my mind screaming profanities directed at my stepfather, but then she nodded her consent. Her trust in me so wholehearted that I felt unworthy, guilt at having brought this hell down upon her tearing me apart inside. But I had to bury it. Feeling guilty wasn't going to get us to safety.

Preparing myself, I gritted my teeth and parted the towel. Keeping my composure steady, outwardly at any rate, I scanned her body for any wounds that looked like they needed immediate attention. In truth, I didn't really know where to begin...her body, so beautiful and feminine, had taken on a patchwork blanket of varying shades of color. Not a limb had gone unscathed. She screamed fragile and broken, and it was all I could do not to crush her to me and refuse to let her go again.

"Where's your first aid kit?" I asked quietly.

"Medicine cabinet"—she paused to yawn and wince simultaneously—"in the bathroom."

"I'll be back," I said, closing the quilt around her.

Hurrying out of the room, I grabbed the first aid kit from the bathroom and headed for the kitchen area, closing the living room window as I passed to shut out the morning chill. Locating the freezer, I hunted out an ice tray and dropped the contents into a cloth. I was gone mere minutes, yet when I returned she was fast asleep, curled in a tight ball at the edge of her bed.

I studied her peaceful form and couldn't bring myself to disturb her too much. Joining her on the bed, I gently pulled her body back to spoon against me and placed the ice against her jaw. She moaned in protest.

"Hush, baby, it will help," I said into her hair, kissing it gently.

She buried her head under my chin and stilled, sleep consuming her once more. She was utterly wiped out.

Now I really didn't know what to do. She desperately needed to rest and I needed to get us out of here before my stepfather hunted us down. But surely half an hour wouldn't hurt? By my reckoning, he wouldn't even know that I was missing yet. I could try and get some rest too. I still felt groggy from the dose the doctor had given me and now that I was lying down, my body relished the comfort.

Nuzzling into her, I closed my eyes and inhaled her freshly-bathed scent, the smell soothing me to the core.

Yes, half an hour would do it and then we could get moving.

I would use the time to plan our next move...

Chapter Eighteen

I BECAME AWARE OF AN incessant buzzing at my ear. The bloody fly persistently irritating me and dragging me out of my peaceful slumber. Groggily, I flapped my hand at the pest only to be rewarded with a shower of water droplets. I groaned and buried my face into the softness of the pillow beneath me to dry it off, curling my body into the warm figure before me as the move prompted a contented feminine sigh...

Emma!

My eyes flew open as realization dawned—I'd fallen asleep! And not for a short while either, if the defrosted makeshift ice pack that had soaked my hand was anything to go by. How could I have been so stupid?

Freeing my arm from Emma's sleepy hold, I lifted my wrist to check the time. We'd been out of it for an hour.

Shit!

The buzzing picked up again; now that I was fully awake it was obvious that it was Emma's doorbell. Rolling out of bed, I shot to the living room window and scanned the street, looking for any sign of who was at the door. I saw my stepfather's car immediately; you couldn't miss the bright red Ferrari on this street. Fear coursed through me, but I tried to tell myself I could handle him. He wouldn't dare hurt me like he had Emma. I just needed to keep him away from her.

I moved to drop the curtain but my hand froze as a new car pulled onto the street. It was Dr Tate!

Now I truly was scared. Why would my stepfather call upon him unless it was to administer meds?

All sorts of horrific thoughts raced through my mind and my stomach churned. I gripped the windowsill and took a steadying breath. I needed to call the cops. There was no way Emma and I were getting out of the apartment block without a fight. And it wouldn't take my stepfather long to decide that the fire escape would give them a route in.

Racing back into the bedroom, I shook Emma awake, panic making me less aware of her wounds, and she yelped as she shot up on the bed.

"Ow! Abi!" she said rubbing at her shoulder, tears pricking at her eyes.

"I'm sorry, baby, but I need your cell. Where is it?"

"In the kitchen, on charge."

I flew into the kitchen, scanning desperately for the phone. Sure enough it was plugged in on the counter. Lunging for it, I almost sent it flying across the room, just managing to rescue it by the charging cable still connected to its bottom. I pulled it up and tugged the cable out, navigating the unfamiliar device for the emergency services dial screen.

"Come on, come on, come on," I mumbled as my nervous fingers took several fumbling attempts to correctly dial out. Finally, I did it, and holding it to my ear I ran back to the bedroom.

"Police," I blurted to the operator when they answered. Then explaining the situation as briefly as I could, I kept watch over Emma. She wasn't moving, she wasn't doing anything. She sat horror-stricken at the edge of the bed, her face ghostly white as she listened to me speak, her blackened body still completely naked.

"Get dressed, baby," I mouthed to her and to my relief, she nodded and started to move.

The buzzing had ceased, which I assumed was because my stepfather was now speaking to Dr Tate. The woman on the other end of the phone was trying to keep me calm but inside I was a mess. She reckoned twenty minutes before the cops would get to us. Could we hold them off for that long?

Poor Emma was struggling to get dressed, her aching limbs refusing to do her bidding as she stepped into a pair of track pants and almost fell. And then the buzzing started up again. At least that meant they were still trying to get in through the front door.

"I need to help my friend," I said to the operator. She asked me to keep on the line and have the phone nearby. "Will do."

I closed the bedroom door, drowning out the incessant sound of the jarring buzzer and placed the cell phone on the side table. Grabbing up a T-shirt from the floor, I turned to Emma. "Here, lift your arms."

Gingerly, she did as I asked and I slipped the fabric over her head—

Crack!

The sound of splintering glass came from the living room. I knew immediately that one of them had come up the fire escape, the persistent buzzing a cunning ploy to distract us from the secondary access one of them had used. We looked at each other and froze, neither daring to move in case we made a sound to draw their attention. My eyes scanned the room trying to find a hiding place.

The closet! It was our only hope to delay things long enough for the police to get here.

Retrieving the cell from the side, I stuffed it in my back pocket and took hold of her hand, pulling her with me to the closet. Opening the door, I was presented with a typical girl's wardrobe, bursting with clothes and boxes, barely room for another item of clothing let alone the two of us.

The sound of footsteps moving around the room next door ended the debate and I nudged Emma forward. She shook her head vehemently, gesturing for me to get in.

Not likely, this was my mess; if anyone was going to get caught, it was me.

Shoving her in, I kissed her lips fleetingly.

"Please stay put...for me," I whispered, and then I closed the door quietly just as the handle turned on the bedroom door.

Pinning myself to the wall behind it, I held my breath.

"Abi? Emma?"

It was Dr Tate.

The intercom buzzer picked up again and he swore. Moving back into the living room, I heard him at the intercom releasing the door for my stepfather and then he unlocked the apartment door, his footsteps now approaching as he resumed his search for us.

"Look, Abi, I know you're here, your car is outside. Why don't you make things easy for everyone concerned and come out?"

I heard him enter the bathroom briefly and then he came back into the bedroom, his back to me as he scanned the room. I looked about me for some form of weapon, anything to swing at his great big head but there was nothing. He took in the strewn contents of the suitcase, the rumpled sheets and then his eyes settled on the closet as he made his way toward it.

"What is it you want?" I said the words quietly, fear making my voice tremble as I tried to avoid looking toward the closet, praying with all my might that Emma would do as I'd asked and stay put.

He spun on his heel before me, his face lifting into a snide grin. "Abi!"

"Nathan?" my stepfather's booming voice made it through the apartment.

"In here," Dr Tate called out and then to me he said, "do you know how much trouble you have caused, young lady?"

Dad strode into the room, his eyes settling on me. "Thank God! Get out there!" he barked.

I refused to move.

"Drug her if you have to," he said turning to Dr Tate, "but it would look better if she made it out of here on her own two feet. What about Emma?"

"I can't find her."

"She has to be here somewhere, *the manipulative little bitch!*" my stepfather cursed, thrusting his hand through his hair and rounding on me. "Clearly the warning from my men wasn't effective if she dared let you come near her again. Where is she, Abi?"

I raised my chin in silent defiance and his eyes flashed dangerously.

"Tell me Abi or I swear"—he raised the back of his hand to me— "I'll beat you myself."

I kept my bold stance, looking anywhere but the closet. Seconds passed, his hand trembling before me and then he withdrew, shoving his hand in his pocket. "Christ! You're your mother's daughter."

"Take her into the living room, Nate, and give her something to make her pliable."

"No!" Emma flew out of the closet, launching herself at Dr Tate. He shifted his body just in time to bypass her move and my stepfather grabbed her, pulling her back kicking and screaming against his chest.

His hand shot to her mouth to muffle her sound and I flipped, diving across the room in a desperate attempt to get her out of his grasp. But Dr Tate moved quickly, grabbing me by the waist to halt my attack.

"Your stepfather has a few things he wishes to discuss with Emma," the doctor said through gritted teeth as he began hauling my rebellious body back into the living room.

My eyes remained fixed on Emma's restrained form through the doorway, sobs racking me from head to foot as I tried desperately to prise his hands off me.

"You mustn't blame your stepfather, Abi," he continued, "he just wants to protect you from bad people like her. Of course, if you had just been a good girl in the first place none of this would have hap—"

"Fuck!" he cursed.

My flailing fist made perfect contact with his groin and he buckled, tossing me onto the couch. Before I could run, he was upon me, one hand pinning me down while the other rummaged around in his bag on the coffee table.

I could hear muffled voices coming from the bedroom and then the sound of skin making contact with skin in a loud crack. My father's angry voice bit back and I realized Emma must have slapped him. He emerged from the room, his cheek blood red, his hand thrust in Emma's hair as he used it to drag her struggling form with him.

They moved to the kitchen and I heard him yanking open drawers. There was the flash of something metal and then they disappeared back into the bedroom, the door slamming shut on Emma's terrified sobbing.

"Don't worry, Abi, he won't kill her, I think your stepfather simply wants to make sure that no man, or woman for that matter, could possibly desire her again."

No! A surge of adrenaline rushed through me, giving me the strength to take him by surprise and make a break for it. I legged it to the bedroom, breaking through the door to find a barely conscious Emma lying on the bed, my stepfather holding her by the neck, the knife mere inches from her face...

"No!" I screamed running forwards just as my stepfather shot to his feet, his hand coming up to hold me back.

"Nate, for God's sake, can't you keep her under control!"

I felt Dr Tate come up behind me, his hands moving around my waist. "Sorry Edward, she's feisty!"

And then he was dragging me out of the room again.

"Emma!" I shouted, trying to get her to move, to fight back, but she didn't even flinch. She lay there completely immobile, her head flopping to one side.

"It will all be better in just a second, Abi," Dr Tate assured me, pausing to lift something off the table and my worst fear was realized as he brought the shiny tip of a syringe toward my neck.

"No, Doctor, no!" I sobbed against him as he used his arm to hold my head off to the side.

"Shh, Abi, don't worry your pretty—"

"Drop it!"

I felt Dr Tate freeze against me. "What the...?"

He turned, keeping me positioned against him, the cold tip of the needle pressing at the taut skin of my neck...

"I said drop it!" An armed cop crouched in the broken window, his pistol trained on Dr Tate. Slowly the doctor lowered the needle but he didn't loosen his grip on me.

The cop kept his eyes fixed on us as he lifted his receiver to speak into it. "All clear."

The front door flew open as two more officers launched into the room, just as my stepfather swung open the bedroom door.

"What the hell is—" He stopped dead as he took in the scene before him.

I felt Dr Tate slacken his grip and I took the opportunity to get free of him, racing past my stepfather and into the bedroom, every thought imaginable running through my mind.

Please let her be okay, please let her be okay...

Emma still lay lifeless on the bed, but there was no blood to be seen. I hurried to her side, pulling her limp body into my arms as I scanned her for further injuries. An officer came in behind me and knelt beside us.

"You okay, ma'am?" he asked, looking to me.

"Yes," I nodded erratically, clinging Emma to me, tears starting to stream down my face. "But her...I don't know...please" My words were coming out a bumbling mess, hysteria well and truly starting to set in, I just couldn't imagine life without her...not my Emma!

Through my blurry vision I could make out him nodding to me, his hands moving expertly over Emma's limp body as he worked to check her vitals.

I was vaguely aware of my stepfather and Dr Tate being read their rights in the next room but all I wanted was for Emma to wake up, to tell me everything was okay, that no one would hurt us again...

I realized the officer had stilled and was speaking to me, his hand on my shoulder as he tried to coax me out of my emotional reverie.

"I'm sorry?" I asked, taking in his reassuring smile with dawning hope.

"She's going to be okay, ma'am," he said. "She looks to have passed out but the ambulance is on its way and they will check you both over properly. Do you understand what I am saying?"

I nodded slowly, the words "she's going to be okay" bouncing around my brain until they finally registered, a surge of relief washing over me and leaving me fuzzy.

"We'll need to take a report from you, but it can wait until you have both been properly checked over. Until then, I suggest you stay in here."

Again, I nodded, grateful that he didn't want me to move, nothing would have made me leave her side right now.

"Look, that's my daughter in there!" I heard my stepfather bellow from the next room, his desperation sending his voice hoarse. "If you just go and get her she will explain that there has been a misunderstanding."

A misunderstanding—not likely!

"Abi! Abi!" he called, "Please get out here and tell them."

"He's right," Dr Tate cut in. "She'll explain all."

I saw red then. The fact that they thought I would seriously bail them out after everything they had done to me...to Emma...and they had the nerve to declare me mentally unfit!

I settled Emma's body back on the bed as I got to my feet, my eyes unable to leave her just yet.

"She's really okay?" I asked the officer, the nagging doubt still there.

"Yes, she'll come to soon enough," he said, his brow creasing with concern as he added, "you know you don't need to go in there?"

I looked from him to the doorway. "I need to do this."

Striding to the doorway, I entered the living area just in time to see them cuffing my stepfather, his hands forced behind his back, his head bowed. Dr Tate was already cuffed and being escorted out by an armed officer. He looked back just as I appeared, the glimmer of relief bright in his eyes as he said, "Here she is now, look, Edward."

My stepfather's head flew up, his face showing a similar glow. "Abi, darling, thank God, please tell them," he said, his head nodding to the officers stood around.

I really couldn't believe they thought me so easily led.

His eyes flitted about the room at my continued silence, his panic swift to resurface. "*Tell them!*"

"Tell them what?" I said coldly. "How you had Emma beaten to a pulp or how you paid a doctor to sedate me and declare me mentally unsound? Or how about the fact you stole my inheritance?"

He froze, the deathlike pallor to his face making him look every one of his advancing years.

"Yes, don't you worry, I'll make sure they know absolutely everything."

Satisfied that I had seen and said enough, I turned to re-enter the bedroom.

"*Abi! Please!*" he implored, his voice cracking. "*How can you do this to me? I have loved you like my own.*"

I looked back at him over my shoulder, the man that had been my father for as long as I can remember, and the anger and hatred that had fueled me over the past twenty-four hours gave way to overwhelming pity. The strength of feeling in his gaze tugged at me, was it really love I saw there? Or was it purely despair that he had finally been caught out?

Ultimately, it didn't matter.

"Goodbye, Edward."

He reacted as though slapped, never before had I addressed him by name. It was a simple, yet effective message to send. And looking back to the sleeping beauty in the bed before me, I pushed him from my mind, just where he belonged. I had far more important things—or rather a far more important someone—to think about now.

Epilogue

MORE ICE, DARLING?"

My sunglass-covered eyes met with her captivating green ones flashing mischievously above me, an ice cube slipping about in her tanned hand as she crouched over my reclined body.

"I wouldn't say no," I said, placing the book I had been reading on the ground next to my sun lounger and giving her my undivided attention.

She smiled, her expression almost childlike with excitement as she lowered the cube to the base of my throat. The ice started melting on contact, the cold water trickling down either side of my neck, the tantalizing sensation making me wriggle with delight.

"Your body is scorching," she said, her voice full of wonder as her head dipped to lap at the water trail she had created.

She continued circling the cube over my skin, across my collarbone, down between my naked breasts and over my torso, all the while her tongue tracing the path left by the ice.

I brought one hand up to play with her free flowing hair as she dipped lower and lower over my body. "If this is what you're going to do every time I have my head in a book, I'm going to read more often."

Her response was to slip her hand beneath the fabric of my bikini bottoms, the intense cold of the melting cube sliding between my folds with such erotic intensity that I bucked beneath her.

"Don't be so cheeky," she murmured against my belly button, her eyes looking up at me suggestively, just as the ice made acute contact with my throbbing clit, the smarting cold making me cry out in a heady mix of pain and pleasure.

My cry echoed around the cliff face into which our secluded villa had been built, a reminder that we could make love where we wanted, when we wanted, and no one would intrude, save for the occasional low flying flight overhead...but that just added to the thrill.

"Nice?" she asked as my lower body became accustomed to the sensation and started to ride the cube of its own accord.

"Always," I said, my head tilting back against the lounger as her mouth crept back up my body, her tongue seeking out one taut nipple and then the other. She worked them both in turn, the buds, already hypersensitive from the heat of the sun's rays, sending thrilling sparks straight to my core and my hands thrusting through her hair, their playful caress forgotten as I encouraged her over me, back and fore...

As the ice in my briefs melted away, the dizzying pressure of her fingers took over, her tempo picking up against me as she worked with the rise and fall of my hips to bring me to the exhilarating heights she never ceased to achieve.

"I will never tire of making you come, baby," she said as she broke away from one nipple to feast at the other.

I moaned my response, incapable of speech, as my body started to tense, the joyous feeling of my climax spreading through every part of me. I arched back as the tide hit, my body pitching beneath her expert fingers, the words tearing from my lips coming straight from the heart, "God, I love you!"

And then her lips were on mine, crushing me in a fierce kiss. Showing me with her actions that she loved me too. I knew she did, even if she hadn't said it. And in my sated state, I was happy to just know it. We were a year into our relationship and it was as tight as ever, my body's response to her as profound as ever. It was enough. For now.

Breaking away, she paused above me, her eyes alight with mischief once more. "Just you remember that when young Daniel visits this evening."

I rolled my eyes at her, the "Daniel thing" had become an age old source of ribbing material for her, used purely for entertainment value since we were all the best of friends these days.

"Young Daniel, as you like to call him, will be in attendance with his beautiful fiancée, or have you forgotten that pertinent fact already?"

"Oh, yes, that's right," she said smiling, "he didn't hang about, did he?"

That made me laugh outright. "Hey, Miss High and Mighty, have you forgotten that we moved in together pretty much straight away."

"That's different," she said with a wave of her hand. I caught it mid-air, bringing her fingers to my lips to press a kiss to each tip, loving how it made her wriggle in anticipation of my next move. Having just made me come, I knew her sexual coil would be wound tight, eager for release, eager for me...

"How so?" I said, slipping one finger into my mouth, my tongue wrapping around it as I sucked gently back.

She gave a small groan. "You know how so."

"Try me..."

"We...*oh!*" she arched her back as I slipped my hand into her briefs, my finger making gentle contact with her swollen nub.

"Continue," I said, my own voice rough with desire as I took in her rising abandon.

"We were made for each other," she breathed, her body moving shamelessly over my hand as she used me to reach her own explosive release. "It was obvious from the start," she added, her glazed eyes making contact with my own, her sincerity in their depths taking my breath away as my heart soared with the words she had used. It was the closest I'd ever been to hearing the words I longed to slip from her lips. We'd had the discussion plenty of times before and it always ended in me parking it. I got that her history meant "I love you" had never been her thing, but I wanted so much for me to be different...to be special.

"*Made for each other*—that sounds like a stamp you might put on Ken and Barbie's backsides," I teased, my mouth dropping to softly kiss at the sensitive underside of her wrist. "Besides, you know full well the pair of them are madly in love."

"Are we back on them?" she asked, struggling to remain on topic.

I nodded at her, easing the pressure of my hand so that I could keep her focus just a bit longer.

"Meanie," she moaned, trying to use her body to coax me back.

"Well, they are utterly besotted," I persisted. "Surely you can see that?"

She nodded, her eyes on me as I started to trail my tongue up the length of her arm, her body obediently relenting to the tempo and pressure I dictated.

"Well, I guess that makes them not so different to us after all..." she remarked thoughtfully.

I stilled, my eyes rocketing to hers, the same question I had asked seconds before leaving my lips, only this time the stakes on this answer were through the roof. "How so?"

She gave me a half-smile, her glittering eyes full of adoration as she brought her hand up to cup my face, her thumb brushing lovingly across my cheekbone. "Because my wonderful, gorgeous Abigail, I am head over heels in love with you."

I didn't have chance to respond as her head lowered to mine, her mouth encouraging my own to part with a gentle nudge as tears welled behind my closed lids, happiness like nothing I had ever known swamping me. I let her guide me into the kiss, from soft and slow, to deep and intoxicating, all the while, the bubble of joy within me feeling fit to burst.

Eventually she broke away, her breathing coming in small, excited pants. "I'm so sorry it took me so long to confess as much."

"Don't apologize, baby," I said, staring up at her with an overwhelming sense of love. "I can't tell you how happy you have made me."

"Then don't tell me..." There was that playful smile again.

"Oh, I'll show you all right," I said, flipping her body so that she lay beneath me on the lounger, my eyes drinking in every inch of her glorious body and loving gaze. *She loves me.*

She really loves me.

Emma: She's perfect, not so pristine, and all mine!

About Rachael Stewart

Rachael Stewart writes love stories, from the heartwarmingly romantic to the wildly erotic! Despite a degree in Business Studies and spending many years in the corporate world, the desire to become an author never waned and it's now her fulltime pleasure, a dream come true. A Welsh lass at heart, she now lives in Yorkshire with her husband and three children, and if she's not glued to her laptop, she's wrapped up in them or enjoying the great outdoors seeking out inspiration.

You can reach her via:
Twitter: @rach_b52
Facebook: rachaelstewartauthor
Website: rachaelstewartauthor.com

Dear Reader,

Thank you for reading *Unshackled*! Many books thrive or perish based on reviews or a lack thereof. Please consider posting an honest review on the site you purchased this book from and/or on Goodreads. If you're new to writing reviews or wouldn't know how to write one, you could start by sharing what you found most enjoyable about this book.

Also, be sure to sign up for the Deep Desires Press newsletter. This is the best way to stay on top of new releases, meet the authors, and take advantage of coupons and deals. Please visit our website at www.deepdesirespress.com and look for the newsletter sign-up box at the bottom of the page.

Thanks again,

Deep Desires Press

WIN FREE BOOKS!

Our email newsletter is the best way to stay on top of all of our new releases, sales, and fantastic giveaways. All you have to do is visit deepdesirespress.com/newsletter and sign up today!

SUBSCRIBE TO OUR PODCAST!

Deep Desires Podcast releases monthly episodes where we talk to your favorite authors—or authors who will soon become your favorite! Find us on Apple Podcasts, Google Play Music, Stitcher, and our website (deepdesirespress.com/podcast/). Subscribe today!

Support the Deep Desires Podcast on Patreon and you can receive free ebooks every month! Find out more at patreon.com/deepdesirespodcast!

Don't Miss These Great Titles from Deep Desires Press

Finding A Keeper
Michelle Geel

When PA Brenna Palmer meets millionaire and sexually unquenchable Gabriel Burke, her search for Mr. Right gets a lot more complicated when he makes her an offer she can't resist.

A scorching hot love story, available in paperback and ebook!

Hot Roast Romance & Coffee Confessions
Jessica Collins, Luna Blue, and Gemma Stone

Quaint cafés, perfectly crafted coffees, and cute baristas are the sources of inspiration for this sexy anthology of coffee shop-themed romances. Jessica Collins, Luna Blue, and Gemma Stone each pen a novella that explores the romances that form over a freshly-brewed cup. From finally finding "the one" to a quick tryst in the stock room, this anthology has it all. It's the perfect accompaniment to a latte and a croissant at your favorite café!

Available now in ebook and paperback!

Stephanie Spicer Erotic Touch Romance
Gemma Stone

Gemma Stone's sexy series follows Stephanie Spicer in her ongoing search for love—and all of the sex she has along that journey. Stephanie is desired by many, both male and female, but she has her heart set on one man. But does that man feel the same about her? Set in the high-stakes world of business, this series is full of sexy fun and lots of drama.

All six novellas are now collected in two anthologies—in both ebook and paperback—with exclusive short stories and author interviews!

Stephanie Spicer's Great Sexpectations—Available Now!

Stephanie Spicer's Great Sexpectations: Volume Two—Available Now!

Going Solo
The Complete "Casual Car Sex" Series Bundle
Storm Stone

When a sexy Las Vegas bad boy finds out that his sex experiences with a mysterious Englishwoman are being used for her blog, he decides to extract his revenge, but it becomes a gateway into their deepest, darkest desires, where there is no turning back...

Available now in ebook and paperback!

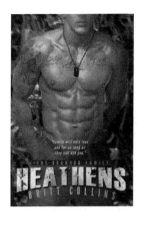

Heathens
Britt Collins

JB, the silent, tatted enforcer of the Branson family, wants to be left alone. No one believes him that the death of his mother is no accident, not even his twin brother Caesar.

The last thing Amina wants or needs is a member of the Branson family complicating her life again. That is, until she sees him—strong, sexy, brooding JB Branson—and her life begins to spin out of control.

Murder, drugs, revenge, along with an overbearing family of criminals; JB and Amina will need each other to stay alive.

Available now in ebook and paperback!

Power To Love
Power Brothers #1
J. Margot Critch

When the Power brothers discover they've inherited a home in Key West, Cash decides to take the opportunity to get away and process his time as a conflict photographer. He gets more than he hoped when he meets Karen Gallagher, an environmental lawyer who needed a break of her own from the stresses of work. What starts as a steamy mile-high encounter may lead to more than either Cash or Karen bargained for. Will Karen and Cash's tryst end in a clean break, or will they leave their hearts in the Florida Keys?

Available now in ebook and paperback!

Stealing Beauty
Jessica Collins

This time, it's the Beast who's going to attempt to tame the Beauty. The only thing he can't protect her from...is himself.

A modern and sexy re-telling of Beauty and the Beast! Available now in ebook and paperback!

Freshman Year
Dalton

What happens in the bedroom freshman year stays with you your entire life.

An anthology of hot sex stories—MF, MM, FF, and more! Available now!

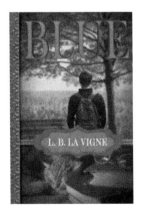

Blue
L.B. La Vigne

A wealthy businessman and rag-tag college student spark up an unlikely romance, but fear of commitment and skeletons from the past threaten their happy ever after.

A sweet (and hot) MM erotic romance— available now in ebook and paperback!

Printed in Great Britain
by Amazon